Never Slow Dance with a Zombie

Never Slow Dance with a Zombie

Never Slow Dance with a Zombie

E. Van Lowe

TOR®

A Tom Doherty Associates Book
New York

NEVER SLOW DANCE WITH A ZOMBIE

A Tor Teen Book
Published by Tom Doherty Associates, LLC
175 Fifth Avenue
New York, NY 10010

www.tor-forge.com

Tor® is a registered trademark of Tom Doherty Associates, LLC.

Library of Congress Cataloging-in-Publication Data

Van Lowe, Ehrich
    Never slow dance with a zombie / E. Van Lowe.—1st ed.
        p. cm.
    "A Tom Doherty Associates book."
    ISBN 978-0-7653-2040-7
    1. Best friends—Fiction. 2. Friendship—Fiction. 3. Zombies—Fiction.
4. Popularity—Fiction. 5. High schools—Fiction. 6. Schools—Fiction.
I. Title.

    PZ7.V2749 Ne 2009
    Fic—dc22

                                                            2009016704

First Edition: September 2009

Printed in the United States of America

0 9 8 7 6 5 4 3 2 1

In memory of Dad, who taught me to love books

Cranford College
3501 Trousdale Parkway
Amherst, MA 01002

Dear Sir or Madam:

If you are reading this letter because you are looking for adventurous, plucky young women who have succeeded in life against all odds yet still found the time to win the heart of the handsome, intelligent, yet sensitive football captain while acing all their classes—you can stop reading now. I am not the future college student you are looking for. To begin with, I hate pluck . . . or spunk, or drive, or initiative. Or any of those words adults use when they're trying to describe the person they'd most like us to be.

Adults have a pretty poor sense of what it's really like in high school. They have no idea of the pressures we're under. For instance, the female lion has pluck. She gets up early in the morning and stalks across the hot Serengeti to hunt for the entire pride. Then, the moment she kills a wildebeest, or an antelope, or something that took a whole lot of effort, along comes a hyena, or some other natural enemy, and steals it from her—just like that. I realize high school is nothing like the Serengeti, but you'd be surprised how many hyenas there are in high school, just waiting to snatch a young lady's kill. So if you're looking for plucky, I am not the student for you.

However, if you are interested in a future college student with more flaws than a casaba melon, but one who is loyal, resourceful, never gives up, and who can learn from her mistakes, please read the enclosed essay. It tells in gory detail of my junior year in high school. It was a year during which I learned many painful personal lessons, not the least of which is why you should never slow dance with a zombie.

Very truly yours,

Margot Jean Johnson

P.S. Adults don't fare very well in my story. If you are a thin-skinned adult, you should throw this in the trash basket immediately!

Chapter
One

 "Do you think I'm a failure?"

"Absolutely," replied Sybil Mulcahy, my best friend in the world since the eighth grade. Or should I say former best friend, considering her response was clearly *not* what I was looking for.

We were in my bedroom studying. Actually, we were pretending to study. For those of you out of the loop, *studying* is teen girl code for talking about boys, parents, siblings, fashion, life—anything but school.

Sybil noticed my brow wrinkling and immediately tried buying her response back. "Wait!" she said. "You fooled me. Usually when you ask me a question the answer is yes. Do I look good in capris? Should I wear pink lipstick? Do you think I'm smart? Am I losing weight? Do you think I'm pretty? Yes, yes, yes, yes, and yes. So, you see? You lulled me into a false sense of yesness. I'm taking my answer back. Ask me again?"

"Forget about it, Syb. You answered truthfully." I rested the heel of my bare foot atop my French book lying on the bed. The books were there in case a parent happened to walk in on our study session. The current session involved painting our toenails.

"No. No, I didn't. Ignore that silly, ludicrous, and ridiculous answer. Now that I'm hearing correctly, my answer is a definite *no, of course not*. You are in no way a failure. What would make you say that, anyway?"

She was sitting on the floor, her back against the bed, applying clear polish to her toes. Sybil rarely used color. She didn't like standing out. She didn't even like the idea of her toenails standing out—go figure.

"Remember this?" I waved the dog-eared sheet of loose-leaf paper I'd recently removed from my box of special things. The box was kept under my bed, away from prying eyes. By *prying eyes* I mean my little creep of a brother, Theo.

"What is it?" Sybil asked without looking up. She continued painting slowly, methodically.

"My high school manifesto," I said as I applied a coat of Firehouse nail polish to my big toe.

I'd written the manifesto the night after middle school graduation. At the time, middle school seemed the low point of my existence. Each day for three long years I attended a school where I was constantly reminded of what a zero I was. I deemed it an experience never to be repeated. Boy, was I ever mistaken. My two years and two months at Salesian High made those middle school years seem like a Disney World vacation.

"I remember," said Sybil, her voice rising. "We were sitting right here, eating snickerdoodles and planning our fabulous high school careers. It was right after graduation, so we didn't even have to pretend we were studying."

She laughed out loud. Normally I would have joined her, but today there was nothing to laugh about.

"Read it," she said. She stopped painting midtoe, and looked at me with anticipation.

I shook my head. "What's the use? I've accomplished nothing on this list."

"Margot, that's ridiculous. I'm sure you've accomplished something. Go on, read it. If you won't, I will." She reached for the page. I yanked it away.

"All right already!" I sighed. I smoothed the wrinkles from the manifesto and read:

My High School Manifesto

I, Margot Jean Johnson, being of sound mind and in front of my best friend, Sybil Mulcahy, and the entire world, hereby decree that my high school experience will far exceed that of junior high.

1. I will be popular

2. I will be more popular than Amanda Culpepper

3. I will be invited to parties

4. I will be invited to more parties than Amanda Culpepper

5. I will have parties that kids will want to go to

    *5a. Amanda Culpepper **will not** be invited*

6. I will have a boyfriend

7. I will have a boyfriend who is cuter than Amanda Culpepper's

8. I will be Homecoming Queen

    8a. Amanda Culpepper, eat your heart out!

9. I will be a cheerleader

~~10. I will have a car~~

10. I will be Prom Queen

11. Amanda Culpepper shall be none of these things

"Wow," said Sybil as I finished reading. "I didn't realize how obsessed you were with Amanda Culpepper back then."

"What are you talking about? I wasn't obsessed with Amanda Culpepper. I couldn't care less about Amanda Culpepper."

She screwed the top back onto the nail polish bottle. "Not obsessed, huh?" she said, eyeing me skeptically.

"No. Of course not."

"Then how come her name is all over your manifesto?"

"I was using her as a benchmark, Syb. I could have used the name . . . oh, Kirsten Dunst, to make my point."

"Riiight," she said, although I'm quite sure she didn't believe me. She changed the subject. "If it makes you feel any better, look at number one on the list. You *are* popular. Remember that time in gym class when we played dodgeball and all the girls, even Amanda, voted you the designated dodger? I do believe it was unanimous."

I stared at her. Was she being serious, or just trying to be nice? Sybil is the Queen of Nice. When I first met her she was standing in front of a bulldozer trying to keep it from plowing over an old tree. She clearly has a tendency to take niceness to unheard-of levels.

"Syb, being unanimously chosen as the person to throw balls at is not my idea of popularity."

"Oh? Okay, I guess I can see that." She again peered at the manifesto. "How about number three? We go to parties. My fifteenth birthday party. What a blast. We danced all night."

It was a slumber party whose exclusive guest list boasted three: me, Sybil, and her cat, Sebastian. We partied the night away to her grandmother's ancient Tom Jones recordings. Didn't she realize how utterly pathetic that sounded? She was obviously being nice. Again!

I read number six: "I will have a boyfriend." I shot her a look that had *failure* written all over it.

"I don't remember that." She took the page from my hand and read it for herself, as if that was going to change things. She looked up at me. "Okay, so no boyfriends, yet. We still have almost two years of high school left. We'll have boyfriends. And not just any boyfriends, Dirk Conrad even."

Dirk Conrad was a six-foot-two senior, with a great body and glacier-blue eyes that made every girl at school ache in her loins. Okay, so maybe nobody got a loin-ache, but you know what I mean. Dirk was hot.

"We can't both go out with Dirk Conrad, Syb."

"I know, silly. I'm using him as a benchmark."

She had to know that the Dirk Conrads of the world wouldn't be caught dead dating my type. And if you're wondering what my type is, let's just say I'm not the type to wind up on the cover of a fashion magazine. Don't get me wrong, I'm not fat. I'm just not skinny. I'm what I like to call an in-betweener.

"I appreciate the sentiment. But I don't think I'm Dirk's type."

"Why not?" She stared at me all wide-eyed and innocent. It was as if Sybil had moved here from Mars three years ago instead of Monrovia, California. She had no idea about high school protocol. A jock like Dirk Conrad, a senior, would never date *me*. Aside from not being Heidi Klum, I wasn't a member of the pool of girls that jocks at our school normally went out with. Unfortunately, Amanda—*gag!*—Culpepper was. Not that I cared.

I did appreciate that Sybil saw me as this amazing person who could run in any circle, fit in anywhere, and do almost anything. But she shouldn't get delusional about it.

"I think you should ask him to go to the carnival Thursday night," she suddenly said.

"Huh? Ask who?"

"Why, Dirk Conrad, of course."

And the delusion continues.

"Are we talking about the real Dirk Conrad or the bench-mark Dirk Conrad? Because the real Dirk Conrad doesn't even know I exist."

"He doesn't know you exist *yet*. But he will." She smiled and leaned in. There was conspiracy in her eyes. "The carnival is a Sadie Hawkins event."

"I know."

"That means girls can ask boys."

"I know."

"His Facebook page says he doesn't have a date yet."

"I know!" Panic was beginning to rise in the pit of my stomach as I realized where the conversation was headed.

"The worst he can say is no."

"Uh-uh! No way!"

Didn't she get what a no from Dirk Conrad could mean? "*No* is a powerful word and not to be taken lightly, Syb. If Amanda and her Twigettes found out Dirk declined my invitation I'd be a laughingstock."

"I thought you weren't obsessed with Amanda."

"I'm not. But there's no sense in inviting ridicule."

"Margot, if we're ever going to make the manifesto a reality we have to start somewhere."

She was right about that. If I was going to keep from being a total high school washout I needed to accomplish something on the list.

"I could get a car," I suddenly said. "That's on the list."

"You crossed it out. I think it was because of how hysterically your father laughed when you ran the idea past him."

"True. He laughed himself into an asthma attack. But now that I'm thinking about it, a car is way more realistic than dating Dirk." I erased the cross-out mark.

"There. Now we've got something to shoot for," I said, brushing eraser crumbs from the manifesto. "You know, I think we should sign up for driver's ed next semester. If I get a car, one of us should know how to drive it."

"What if I ask him for you?"

Instinctively I stiffened. Was I hearing correctly? "Why would you do that?"

"We're best friends, Margot. And I *know* you'd like to go out with him."

"Well . . . yeah." I swallowed hard.

"There you have it. What are best friends for if not to do cool stuff for each other?"

Some days it seemed as if Sybil really was from Mars. Best friends rarely do cool stuff for each other at our age. High school is where best friends sometimes stab each other in the back.

"What do you think?" she asked, smiling up at me.

What I thought was, *No Earth girl can be this naive.* But of course, I didn't say that. At first, I was going to remind her that she was as shy as I was when it came to boys—shyer even. But all of a sudden, I was finding it hard to concentrate. The idea of going to the carnival with Dirk had invaded my thoughts. And I have to admit, I liked the invasion.

"And you don't have to worry about any embarrassment," she continued. "If he says no, he'll be saying no to me."

"But why would he say yes? He doesn't even know me."

"Dirk is so cute, I'll bet every girl at school is afraid to ask him out. They're probably all thinking, *He'll never go to the carnival with me.*"

"That's pretty much what I was thinking."

"I know, but don't you see? Poor Dirk will probably spend Thursday night home alone because everyone is too chicken to ask him out. . . . Everyone, but you."

Her argument was making sense. Still, I had my doubts. "I don't know, Syb. . . ."

"Imagine the look on Amanda Culpepper's face when you show up at the carnival with Dirk."

And just like that, I didn't have so many doubts.

"Amanda and her twigs will be sooo jealous," she sang.

Amanda Culpepper jealous of me?

This was worth considering.

 The following morning I still couldn't get the thought of Amanda being jealous of me off my mind. I imagined her envious eyes following as I strolled the carnival grounds on Dirk's arm. The thought had me giddy with delight.

Sybil and I were halfway through the fifteen-block walk to school. We rarely took the bus. The bus was divided into cliques, and was yet another reminder of my failure. The cliques included Amanda and her twigs—a.k.a. the Twigettes or it-girls; the Goths; the emos; the jocks; the girl jocks—a.k.a. girls who think skintight warmup suits with writing on the butt and matching tennis shoes are cute (they're not); the preps (rich kids headed for the Ivy League); the stoners; and lastly the stoner nerds. Stoner nerds are kids who think getting stoned will make them cool. It won't. A nerd is a nerd. When Sybil and I rode the bus there was a ninth clique: two cute girls who were too cool to be subjected to this junk—us.

"Cliques are so unnecessary," said Sybil as we walked.

"I know" was all I could muster. The school's cliques were

Sybil's one pet peeve. Normally I'd indulge her outrage, but today I was too excited to even fake it.

"You never really gave me an answer last night," she suddenly said.

"Answer? About what?" Yes, I know it's the only thing I'd been thinking about. But I've got my pride.

We were crossing Maple Street when Sybil stopped and eyed me knowingly. "Margot, this is me. I know you've been thinking about it."

"All right, you got me. I can't get it off my mind."

"And?"

And why not ask Dirk out? I thought. If he says yes—hallelujah. If he says no, it would be a request from some strange girl he'd probably never remember. I would be shielded from all embarrassment. I envisioned me and Dirk at the carnival, riding rides, eating cotton candy, holding hands. There was a third person in that imagined picture that made it seem perfect—a person whose jealous eyes would be on me all night.

"All right," I finally said. "Let's do it."

Sybil smiled.

I smiled; then I mentally began preparing myself for gym class, or as I like to call it, forty-five minutes of hell.

"Margot Jean Johnson!" Mrs. Mars, my gym teacher, bellowed in her deep, hoarse tone. "I don't care how many notes you bring from home. If you don't pass the state endurance exam you are failing PE, young lady." She waved my most recent excuse note in my face.

I was very proud of that note. It was my best creative effort so far:

Dear Mrs. Mars,

Please excuse our daughter and the apple of our eye,
Margot, from participating in gym class today. We had
dinner at Captain Pete's last night where she accidentally
swallowed a fish bone, and we fear all that running and
jumping you force the kids to do may cause her to puncture
a lung.

> *Sincerely,*
> *Mrs. Trudi Johnson*

"Ow, ow, ow!" I screeched from my perch atop the bleachers where all the girls with notes sat. I clutched at my chest. "Physical activity could kill me." I coughed feebly for effect.

"Poppycock!" snarled Mrs. Mars. "You'll pass the state endurance exam, or you'll be right back here next semester. Same bat time, same bat channel."

Mrs. Mars was the gym teacher from hell, an ancient leftover from the seventies when breaking rocks with sledgehammers was considered exercise. She dressed in long pleated skirts and industrial-strength tennis shoes as if she were teaching gym class in Bulgaria. Her hair was cinched back into a tight bun, and around her neck she wore a hideous blue scarf. While she may have thought of it as a fashion statement, I was certain the scarf was there to hide the chicken skin that rippled along her throat.

"I want to work out, I really do. But I'm all my parents have got."

A few snickers erupted from the group on the gym floor. I stiffened, knowing who they were from. My eyes moved to Amanda Culpepper and her crew. Amanda tossed back a lock of blond hair and smirked in my direction. She and her crew were already in their gym uniforms.

The uniforms were hideous, puke-green monstrosities that billowed on our frames like sails, making most of us look like Spanish galleons, sailing across the gym floor in search of treasure—or a decent change of clothes. Yet somehow Amanda managed to look cute in hers. The uniform didn't billow on her frame at all. *I bet she starches hers.* I find it hard to like someone who can look cute in a gym uniform.

"Margot Jean Johnson," Mrs. Mars called, dragging my attention back. She cocked her head to one side. "I don't care if you are your parents' last hope. Tomorrow morning, note or not, we start getting you in shape."

"But—"

"That will give us just enough time to get you ready for the state endurance exam. So, tomorrow you're mine, same bat time, same bat channel." And then she chuckled, as if she'd said something funny.

It was sad really, knowing that a woman entrusted with the lives of so many young people couldn't care less if I lived or died. But I sucked it up. Mrs. Mars, or even Amanda Culpepper, couldn't ruin my day. I was going to ask Dirk to the carnival with me. Okay, I wasn't going to ask him—Sybil was going to do the asking—but if he said yes he'd be saying yes to me.

Later, as Sybil and I approached our lockers we saw him—Dirk Conrad, standing alone putting some books in his locker, and looking oh-so handsome. Dirk had already distinguished himself as the best player on the varsity basketball team, and was a finalist at last year's science fair. He was cute, tall, intelligent—everything I wanted in a boy. I was suddenly finding it hard to breathe.

Sybil glanced at me. "Are you okay?"

"Yes. It's . . . hot in here." My palms began to sweat and itch as if I'd rubbed them in a patch of poison ivy. A lump formed in my throat. I don't know how I managed to speak. "Well . . . there's Dirk." The words crawled from my throat.

"I see him." She glanced over at him for like a nanosecond before turning her attention back to her locker.

"What are you waiting for?" I nudged her in his direction. He was twenty feet from us, wearing a gray varsity jacket that highlighted the blue of his eyes.

"Margot, you're standing right here. Am I supposed to walk over to him and say, 'Hey, my friend over there wants to go to the carnival with you'?"

Yes, I thought. But I knew that's not what she was looking for. "No, no, of course not," I replied. "I was merely bringing to your attention that he's standing just twenty feet away."

"I see that, Margot."

Note to self: Picking up on hints is not one of Sybil's strong suits.

"Okay, so what's the plan?" I asked, eager to hear the clever scheme she'd concocted for approaching him and popping the question.

"Dirk is in my World History class and you're not. I'll go up to him right after History."

"And?"

"And ask him if he wants to go out with you."

So much for ingenuity.

"After History?" I said, screwing up my face. "Then I won't get to see the expression on his face when you say my name."

"I know."

"I won't see if his eyes fill with bliss or horror."

"I know."

"History is eighth period. I'll have to wait ALL DAY."

"I know!"

Dirk finished at his locker and moved away. He didn't

glance in our direction. My doubts about the whole dating thing returned.

"Sybil, I've been thinking, maybe I should ask him myself."

"Oh, no! You're just trying to get out of it. Remember the manifesto? Boyfriends?"

"Yeah," I said weakly. "But we're just two months into our junior year. We've got loads of time."

"Margot, just let me do this for you, okay? I'm your best friend. I won't mess it up."

I wasn't worried about her messing it up. Dirk hadn't looked in my direction. We were a mere twenty feet away and I didn't even rate a glance. I realized then that even if he said no to Sybil, the embarrassment would still be mine to bear.

"Okay. Do it," I said with a sigh. But my mind conjured up the husky voice of Mrs. Mars saying, "This is a mistake, Margot Jean Johnson. A big, fat mistake."

Chapter
Three

 And now a brief note about text messaging: Texting is one of the greatest inventions of all time, right up there with the vaccine for polio and the mosquito ring tone. For it allows us to stay on top of important, life-altering issues while going through our mundane school day.

Sybil, unfortunately, is unappreciative of this great invention. I texted her midway through eighth period:

PCM

Please call me. A simple OK would have done, but Sybil didn't respond. How rude! I know she got it. And I know she knows I know she got it. It's hard enough concentrating at the end of the day. Sybil was forcing me to concentrate on French with my social life hanging in the balance.

My French teacher, Mr. Monsieur—which is obviously a fake name—saw me looking into my lap, frantically typing into my phone.

"*Margot, comment vas-tu?*" which is French for "stop tex-ting and pay attention."

"I'm fine. *Très bien*," I replied, and smiled. I threw in that tiny bit of French hoping he'd think I *was* paying attention and move on to the next student. My ploy did not work.

"Good," he said. "Would you please come up to the board and write the following sentence *en français?*" But of course he said the entire thing in French, and while I wasn't able to fol-low along word for word, I knew exactly what he meant: It was time for Margot Jean Johnson's public humiliation.

"*Merci beaucoup*," I said as I got up. There were a few re-lieved snickers from classmates who breathed sighs of relief over dodging the chalkboard assignment bullet. I moved to the board, my mind racing.

"Mr. Monsieur, before we begin I want to thank you for having such a profound effect on my life." I delivered this with such sincerity that a blank expression actually crossed his face. He was trying to figure out if I was serious or yank-ing his chain. For my part I was buying time, hoping I could come up with a clever reason why I couldn't do the assign-ment today: *I'm sorry, sir, but as much as I'd love to do the sentence, I'm afraid I've been stricken with a sudden case of hysterical blindness. Can someone please help me back to my seat?*

I wish someone would explain to teachers that embarrass-ing us in front of twenty-two of our peers does nothing toward helping us learn. In fact, it has the opposite effect. Teachers should call on the kids who actually *want* to go up to the board. You know, those kids with their noses so far up the teachers' butts they can tell what they had for lunch. I know, gross—but I'm trying to make a point. Why call on those of us who are doing our best to blend into the woodwork?

"Mademoiselle Johnson," Mr. Monsieur said, his eyes urging me on.

As I started writing, I tried glancing surreptitiously at my phone. Still nothing from Sybil.

"Mademoiselle Johnson, ce qui est dans votre main?"

"Um. Okay, you're asking me a question . . . and it's in French, right?"

A few snickers from the class as Mr. Monsieur's brow pinched tight. "I asked, 'What is in your hand?'"

"Oh. Easy. *La bibliothèque.*"

"Ahh. So, that's the library in your hand, is it?"

The class erupted with laughter.

I looked around the room, my cheeks flushed, one thought on my mind: *I'm going to kill Sybil.*

"I hope you're happy!" I said when she finally arrived at our lockers. "I totally messed up in French, and now I've got an extra dose of homework, and it's all your fault." Class had been out for fifteen minutes. I'd been waiting by my locker, stress lines snaking across my brow. "Where were you?" I slammed open my locker and rummaged around for my French workbook.

"I was in history class." She had this silly half smile playing on her lips.

"I texted you three times!"

"Five, but who's counting."

"Well?" I found the workbook and stuffed it in my backpack.

"Well, what?"

I know she thought she was being cute and funny, drawing out the tension of the moment. But she was actually being ridiculously childish.

I took a deep, cleansing breath. "Did you happen to speak with Dirk?" I was calm on the outside, but my insides were churning as if they'd been thrown into a blender.

"Yes."

"And how did it go?" I wanted to wipe that silly grin right off her face—but I played it cool and smiled back as I eased my locker shut.

"Well . . . I said if he wasn't doing anything tomorrow night, my very good friend, you, would love to go to the carnival with him. And he said . . . maybe. He'd think about it." She was grinning from ear to ear.

Maybe? Maybe! I couldn't believe my ears.

"He didn't say no?" I stammered.

"I know."

"He didn't say 'Margot? Who's Margot?' "

"I know."

"He didn't say 'I'd rather stick needles in my eyes.' He didn't say 'Please! I'm going to the carnival with Amanda Culpepper.' He said 'Maybe.' *Maybe!*" At that moment my earlier embarrassment in French didn't seem so bad, as the possibility of going to the carnival with Dirk once again danced in my head.

For those of you out of the loop, the word *maybe* is teen boy code for *I don't have a girlfriend right now, and while I may have been asked out by someone else, going out with you sounds like a good idea, too. I just need a little time to think about it.* You've got to admire boys. They can pack a lot into one word.

I was beside myself with the possibility. Sybil said she'd come over after dinner and we'd call him about the "homework."

Later, at home, I again pulled out my high school manifesto and reread my lofty goals: *I will be popular; I will go to parties; I will have a boyfriend.*

Suddenly those things didn't seem so unattainable. Dirk and I would go to the carnival and I'd laugh at his jokes and he'd tell me how cute my eyes are when they're crinkled with laughter. Then I'd tell him how fond I am of basketball, which isn't a total lie because I have a real appreciation for boys in shorts. And he'll say how fond he is of girls with meat on their bones, which only makes sense since I can't imagine any boy wanting to go out with a girl just to watch her dine on a grape. And everyone at school will say what a cute couple we are, and we'll be invited to all the *in* parties, but we'll only attend a few, because we'll want to spend most of our free time alone together.

Perfect, I thought. Having a boyfriend was the first step. My high school manifesto was about to become a reality.

At dinner that night I daydreamed about what it would be like having Dirk over for dinner, sitting with my family, playing footsie with me under the table, talking, laughing, sharing his thoughts of the day. Unfortunately, there's a person who shows up at our dinner table every night who'd make that dining experience a total nightmare—my ten-year-old brother, Theo.

I'm sure there are lots of girls who enjoy their younger sibling's youthful antics. I do not happen to be one of them.

"I don't like chicken!" Theo whined as he dumped most of the mashed potatoes from the serving bowl onto his plate.

"Oh, really," I said. "Then why are there *two* chicken wings on your plate? If *I* didn't like chicken *I'd* leave that extra wing for somebody who might appreciate it."

"I like wings," he snarled as he inhaled the first. "They're not really chicken. Wings are fun food."

"I like wings, too," I said. "I'm sure we all like wings, don't we?" I threw a look at my parents for confirmation. They looked away.

If Dirk were here he'd back me up.

I turned back to Theo. "Unfortunately chickens are only born with *two* wings," I said as if talking to a three-year-old. My cheeks reddened as my patience slipped away. Even thoughts of Dirk couldn't mask the fact my little brother was an idiot.

"I know they have two wings," Theo said, a goofy smirk playing on his lips. He waved the second wing under my nose like a maestro teasing the air with his baton. Then he devoured it, slurping the meat off the bone like a human vacuum cleaner. "All gone," he sang as he hoisted the meatless bone above his head as if it were a trophy.

I shot my mother an exasperated glance.

"You two be nice," is all she said. But what she meant was, *You know we always let your little creep of a brother get away with everything; suck it up and grab a thigh!*

I looked over at my father, who again avoided my gaze. He scooped tiny spoonfuls of food onto his plate, pretending life with my brother was as normal as the sunrise. A part of me felt sorry for my parents. They had to know that having my brother was the biggest mistake of their lives. If only they'd stopped with me. I'm not saying I'm perfect. But at least I'm not a total embarrassment. I know, some of you are thinking, *How embarrassing could it be?* Obviously you don't have a little brother whose greatest gift is taking a mouthful of PB&J and squirting it out his left nostril while humming the theme to *Skunk Fu!* . . . I'm not kidding.

To deal with their misery my parents pretend our lives are normal. But I'm sure if I ever listened at their bedroom door in the middle of the night, I'd hear them crying their eyes out over their humongous mistake. By the way, I'd never listen at my parents' bedroom door. That's disgusting.

The doorbell rang.

"I'll get it," hollered Theo.

I jumped up. "It's not for you, you little creep! It's Sybil." I shot an imploring look at my mother.

"Theo, finish your dinner," she said, and smiled at me. Finally some justice.

I let Sybil in, and we went right to my room to make the call.

"What are you going to say to him?" I asked as she punched in Dirk's number.

"We'll ask him about the homework, of course."

"Right, right." I'd forgotten that calling a boy and asking about the homework is a teen girl excuse for calling said boy and talking about anything her heart desires. You don't even need to have a class with a boy to discuss *homework*. Teen code is so cool. I don't know what I'm going to do when I turn twenty.

"Hello?" Dirk's smooth, sexy voice came on the line. Sybil held the phone between us. I could hear him breathing on the other end. He even breathed sexy.

"Say something," she whispered.

"Huh? You say something."

"He's *your* date."

"Hellooo?" he repeated.

"But he's not in any of my classes."

"It's not homework, Margot, it's *homework*."

"Who is this? I can hear you talking, you know."

Sybil eyed me, her lips defiant and tight. It was clear she wasn't going to talk to him. "Umm. *Parlez-vous français?*" The French words crept from my throat. Why I chose a language I could hardly speak I have no idea. I just panicked.

Sybil's eyes widened. "What are you doing? Talk to him in English. He's not going to bite."

"Who is this? Is this some kind of joke?" Dirk demanded.

"Umm, no. No speaky English," I said, and quickly hung up.

Sybil glared at me. "Margot, I made the opening for you. You're going to have to talk to him."

"I know. But I thought you were going to do all the talking this time. You know, tell him what a wonderful person I am and how he was so lucky to be going out with me, while I listened in. Why did you spring him on me like that?"

"Because I knew if I didn't, you'd make some lame excuse why you couldn't talk. And I'm not going to let you blow this opportunity."

"Oh." After a moment I sighed. She knew me too well. "You're right. I just need to work up to it, that's all."

The tension lines around her eyes relaxed. She smiled. "I know you will. Tomorrow."

Suddenly, I was into it. "Yes! Tomorrow I'll show up at school everywhere that Dirk might be, looking ravishing. I'll smile and casually wave in a way that lets him know I'm fun and intelligent but not clingy. No talking involved in that."

It's amazing how much a girl can convey in a smile. Of course, if a girl was, say, shallow and brainless as a tick, her smile would convey that as well. Unfortunately some boys like the brainless type, which is why Amanda and the Twigettes always seem to have boyfriends. But Dirk was different. Any boy who was an athlete *and* a finalist in the science fair was way too complicated for Amanda's bunch.

"Sounds like a plan," Sybil replied. "Tomorrow we turn that *maybe* into a *yes*."

Chapter
Four

The next morning I pulled out the snug-fitting top I'd bought myself for my birthday, along with a pair of black slacks that did wonders to hide my huge thighs. My father once called the top too revealing—which is exactly what I was going for. It's a simple law of nature that when fishing, no matter how smart the fish, to attract the fish, you need something flashy.

"Flashy enough?" I asked Sybil, who had come over early to help me pick out the perfect outfit.

She nodded. "Here, put this on," she said, handing me her coveted bottle of Heavenly Heart by Clinique. A birthday gift from me. When I bought the cologne I was hoping she'd let me splash some on every once in a while. *Yes!*

"I've often wondered about fragrance as a gift," I said as I dabbed a bit in the center of my chest. "I mean, what is the buyer thinking when they choose a fragrance: 'This smells lovely, it's perfect for so-and-so,' or 'So-and-so stinks like poop! I hope this helps.'" She looked at me, her eyes narrowing.

"Obviously I was thinking the former when I bought it for you. . . . I'm sorry. I'm just making conversation."

She laughed lightly. "Margot, I know you're nervous." Her tone was understanding.

"Tell me about it," I replied as I looked myself over in the mirror.

"Stop worrying. You look great."

I did look great. The moment of truth had arrived. My outfit, my wave, my smile, my scent were all ready to be put to the test. The only thing left to do was be in the right place at the right time.

"Hi, Dirk!"

Sybil and I were standing near our lockers when Dirk made his first appearance of the day. My heart practically leaped into my mouth when I saw him. He was so cute, cuter than the last time I saw him. My palms were again sweaty, my arms felt as if they'd been tied down by a sack of bricks, and my tongue was covered by a huge, woolen overcoat—which is probably why I got tongue-tied and my "Hi Dirk" came out "Lie Lirk."

Dirk looked in our direction, puzzled at first, then seeing me he smiled and waved. A few moments later he was finished at his locker and gone.

"Wow," I said, as relief drained all the tension from my body. "That wasn't so bad."

"I know. And you almost spoke to him in English this time."

"And he . . . smiled at me."

"I know," Sybil said.

"He *waved* at me."

"I know."

"He . . . might say yes and go to the carnival with me tonight."

"I know!"

"Okay. The next time I see him today, I talk to him—in English."

"Oooh," Sybil said with a playful smile.

Just then the morning announcement came over the PA system.

"A terrific Thursday morning to the students of Salesian High . . ." Principal Taft always started the day's announcement with one of his corny greetings—miraculous Monday, terrific Tuesday, wonderful Wednesday—before going over the day's events. The student body dutifully stopped whatever they were doing each morning to listen. This morning's announcement ended with Principal Taft reminding us that: ". . . tonight is Salesian High night at the carnival. Let's have a big Salesian Knight turnout."

A boyfriend, popularity, cool parties were within my grasp. All I needed to do to start the ball rolling was talk to Dirk about going to the carnival with me tonight, and turn his maybe into a yes.

The day started out perfectly; then Amanda Culpepper and her band of bones swept into the corridor like an ill wind. Her locker was a few feet from where we were standing, but if you weren't a member of Amanda's crew or the object of amusement, she had a way of looking through you as if you didn't exist.

"Oh, and did you see what she had the nerve to wear to school this morning?" Amanda crooned to her entourage. Then she laughed the laugh of a thousand cuts. I had been wounded by it before. But I was feeling too good about myself to allow Amanda's snotty attitude to get to me today.

As Sybil and I moved away from our lockers, Amanda dropped her World History book. Without thinking, I stooped and picked it up. It was a reflex that surprised even me.

As I handed her the book her eyes moved to me. The words *amusement* and *derision* winged through my mind.

"Here ya go," I said, not knowing what to expect.

She looked me up and down as if seeing me for the first time. "Um . . . Okay." She took the book, and the moment it was out of my hand I once again became invisible to her. *Good*, I thought. *Better to be invisible than laughed at*. She turned her attention back to her friends and continued her conversation as Sybil and I moved on.

"She didn't even say thank you," Sybil groused.

"Didn't she?"

"No, she didn't."

Sybil was too busy being angry to hear the laugh of a thousand cuts as it wafted up the hall. But I heard it, and knew it was directed at me.

Chapter
Five

Sybil gave me a detailed schedule of Dirk's where-abouts throughout the day. His first-period class was in room 101. I needed to be standing just outside his door when class let out. But there was one problem. My first-period class this morning was Geometry—*yech!*—in room 334. If I stayed in class until the bell rang I'd never make it down three flights of stairs and over to the other side of the building in time. I needed to be let out of class ten minutes early.

My Geometry teacher, Mr. Porter, reminded me of a drill sergeant from an old army movie. He was trim and proper, and wore crisp white shirts and khakis. He strutted around the room like he was God's gift to geometry, spouting all kinds of postulates and theorems to let us know he was smarter than we were. *Hello! You're the teacher. If you're not smarter than a bunch of eleventh-graders we're in trouble.* He was the kind of teacher who could listen to himself talk all period long, which normally was okay with me. But today I had to interrupt. I raised my hand, catching him mid-drone.

"Um, excuse me. But can I be excused?"

He looked at me, annoyed. "I'm sure you can hold it for ten minutes, Miss Johnson." He was about to drone on.

"Actually, sir, I can't. You see, well, it's kind of *personal*. But if you must know, I can come up and explain it in private." I held my stomach for effect.

Mr. Porter's cheeks began to redden with embarrassment. "Are you going to be all right?"

"Yes," I said softly, still holding my stomach. "I just need . . ." I let the sentence hang in the air.

"Yes, yes," he said quickly. "Of course. And don't worry about the homework assignment. I'll have one of your classmates get it to you."

"Thanks," I whispered as I gathered my things.

Male teachers are so easy. All a girl has to do is hold her stomach and use the *P* word and they'll hustle her out of the room so fast her head will spin. A teacher is an authority figure. You'd think he'd want to know what's going on. But not when we use the *P* word. Teachers hate looking dumb, and all men become babbling idiots when a female says anything about that area south of her belly button.

One time my mother hinted that my father should pick up a feminine product for her while he was at the store. You'd have thought he was having a heart attack. His face turned a deep crimson and he began stammering and stuttering as if he'd lost the ability to form a coherent sentence.

I don't get it. It's as if we had the world's most complicated jigsaw puzzle below our waists, or a whole season's worth of *Jeopardy* questions. Anyway, the *P* word is a girl's most powerful weapon against male teachers, and I used it with impunity.

I reached room 101 just as the bell rang, and waited, holding my breath until I saw Dirk exiting the room. Then I zoomed forward, barreling straight into him. My books went flying.

"Oh, my goodness," I said.

"Sorry," he said. "I didn't see you."

What a gentleman. It was obviously *me* that ran into *him*.

"Oh, it's you," I said.

"Yeah," he said.

"Wow," I said.

"Yeah, wow," he said.

"Go figure," I said.

"Yeah," he said again.

Okay, I know, normally I'd say this was an insipid conversation suited for three-year-olds who'd been dropped on their heads one too many times. And yet that day it was poetic. He helped me gather my books.

"The carnival's tonight," I said.

"Yeah," he said for the fourth time in like thirty seconds. "Should be fun."

"I agree. . . ." Did he just ask me on a date? Was that some kind of cool boy code for "I want to go out with you"? Face it, no boy as cool as Dirk is going to come right out and say "Come to the carnival with me." And since I'd never been asked on a date before—at least, not by anyone who counts—I didn't know what he was supposed to say. Dirk handed me my books and moved away, leaving me staring after him confused.

"What do you think?" I asked Sybil, who was in my second-period class.

"Sounds like he helped you pick up your books."

"I know that. But he said 'Should be fun.' Why would he say that if he didn't want to go out with me?"

"Margot, are you listening to yourself? Since when does 'Should be fun' mean 'Let's go out'?"

"How many boys have asked you on a date?" I snarled. "And your cousin Thomas and that runny-nosed seventh-grader don't count!"

"What's that supposed to mean?"

"It means cool boys don't just come out and say it."

"Margot, I don't want to argue with you. I want this to happen as much as you do."

Her words stopped me. She was being nice again. I looked into her earnest, blue eyes. They were filled with concern.

She is truly from another planet, I thought. Even Mother Teresa wasn't *this* nice.

I sighed. "The carnival's cool and all, but it's really no biggie."

And now a brief note about lying to your best friend: A girl's best friend is rarely her *best* friend. That's because she's the last person a girl can trust with her innermost feelings. Best friends are the people we're most vulnerable to. And since we girls spend half our time snarking at and attacking each other, our best friends are the last people we want to trust with personal information they can drag out of the closet and use against us one day. Face it, we'd give some of our most precious information to our enemies before we gave it to our friends. And that's sick! Boys don't have this problem.

Back to me and Sybil.

"Margot, before we jump to any conclusions about Dirk, let's be sure," she said patiently.

Sybil was right. I was getting ahead of myself. There was only one way to get to the bottom of this. I needed to run into Dirk during next period and continue the conversation. I consulted his schedule. I noted that Dirk stopped by his locker between third and fourth periods at precisely 10:51 A.M. Sybil and I synchronized our watches. Today we'd be there waiting for him.

"What are you going to say?" asked Sybil. We'd rushed to our lockers as soon as the bell rang.

"I don't know." My mind searched for an answer. "If I ask him 'What should I wear?' and I'm wrong about the date, he'll look at me like I've just grown two heads and never speak to me again. If I say, 'Were you asking me out?' and he *was* asking me out, he'll think I'm such an idiot geek he'll change his mind about dating me forever."

"Margot, calm down. You're over-thinking this."

"You're right," I said.

Time passed and Dirk didn't show. Just when we thought he wasn't coming I heard someone sing, "There she is, Miss Americaaaa."

I wheeled around. Baron Chomsky stood smiling at me.

Baron Chomsky wasn't the biggest geek at Salesian High. That distinction belonged to Milton Sharp, who had a 4.0 GPA and wore goofy T-shirts with cartoon characters no one had ever seen or heard of on the front. But while Baron Chomsky wasn't the biggest geek at Salesian, he was the *only* geek at Salesian who professed his undying love for me—*gag!*

I scanned the corridor hoping to discover it was Dirk who had been singing. No such luck.

"I'm busy, Baron," I said with as much disdain as I could muster.

"I know—busy being beautiful." His voice rang out loud enough for everyone in the corridor to hear.

Oh ... my ... God!

This was the kind of thing that made Baron's loving me so

intolerable. He couldn't do it in private. No siree. Baron was a first-rate exhibitionist who'd rather make a big public display of his unwanted affection than slip me a secretive note between classes. Posters, banners, and an oversized birthday card with a large photo of him on the front hung on my locker—that was Baron's style.

Last February for Valentine's Day he had come into my English class dressed as a blues singer—dark glasses, a stingy-brimmed hat, and a guitar. He sang "Margot Done Stole My Soul," an original composition about me being a master thief who had snuck up on him in the middle of the night and stolen his affection. Total embarrassment.

"I don't think he's coming," Sybil said, rolling her eyes at Baron.

"I'm right here. How do you want me?" He leaned casually against the locker. "Shaken, not stirred," he said in a phony British accent that was supposed to make him sound like James Bond. It didn't. He sounded like a geek with a phony British accent.

Just then the first bell rang. 10:55 A.M.

"We better go before we're late," said Sybil.

"Yeah," I replied sadly. "Good-bye, Baron," I said, and we moved away. I again checked Dirk's schedule. "Looks like our next chance is right after gym class."

"Margot, if you want to go to the carnival with Dirk, we've got to do this today."

"I know," I said. "We will." I tried telling myself, *You have lots of time.* But I could feel my golden opportunity slipping slowly away.

In gym class my day took a turn for the worse. Mrs. Mars was waiting for me.

"Margot Jean Johnson, put on your gym uniform and get

ready to work out. Today you are mine," she rasped in her gruff, throaty tone.

"But I have a note."

"No notes today, remember? Today we work." I was so caught up in the dating drama I'd totally forgotten her threat.

"But I'm really, really not well."

She sighed. "What is it this time, life-threatening hangnail?"

Just then I swooned, my knees buckling as I almost dropped to the floor. I flung the back of my hand against my forehead for effect. "Oooh!"

"Oh, for crying out loud. Let me see the note."

She plucked the note from my hand and read:

Dear Mrs. Mars,
Please excuse our only daughter and heir, Margot, from participating in gym class today. She woke up with a 102 temperature. We sent her to school because we understand the importance of education. But we are concerned if she participates in gym her temperature may go even higher and that could cause brain damage, which would make it impossible for her to get into a good college.
                    Sincerely,
                    Mrs. Trudi Johnson

Mrs. Mars finished the note and chuckled. "Very creative. Tell your mother bravo." Her eyes turned serious. "Now get into uniform."

"But . . . but . . ." I took a few steps back. I couldn't work out—not today. I couldn't risk sweating my hair into a frizzy poofball the day of my big date. "Feel my forehead," I demanded.

"No, thank you. I've been around long enough to know the old hot-water-on-the-forehead-just-before-class trick."

Hmm. I didn't know that one. I logged the info for future reference.

"But you can get in serious trouble for ignoring a note from a parent. And what if I die!" I was truly getting agitated.

"That'll be my cross to bear. Now get dressed."

I hate to waste a good note, but it was clear she wasn't giving in today. "Okay," I said with a resigned sigh. "What are we doing today?" I prayed it wouldn't be something athletic.

"Dodgeball," she wheezed.

"Great! I love dodgeball," called Sybil.

I shot her a look that could kill. "I'm sure you do."

In the locker room, as I slipped into my hideous green gym uniform, I noticed that Amanda was looking at me, not through me like she normally did, and gesturing as she spoke to the Twigettes. Then she started across the room.

Amanda coming toward me meant just one thing—humiliation. *What could she possibly want with me?* Then I remembered that we were playing dodgeball. *I am not going to be her designated dodger*, I told myself as she approached. But something in her eyes, the half smile on her lips, said that wasn't why she was coming over. My head started spinning as I shuffled through the reasons she'd be talking to me after all these years.

Was it to apologize once and for all about seventh-grade summer camp?

This was something that had haunted me ever since the incident all those years ago.

"Um, Margot, right?"

As if she didn't know. "Yes. That's me. What's up?"

"Um, are you stalking my boyfriend?"

My breath caught in my chest. "Boyfriend?"

"Dirk tells me you've been turning up everywhere he's been. I'm sure it's not a coincidence. You need to stop."

My body suddenly stiffened as though rigor mortis was setting in. I couldn't move.

"D-Dirk?" The name struggled from my lips.

"Dirk Conrad, my *boyfriend*!"

Somehow I forced out a tiny laugh. "Ha, ha. Dirk Conrad thinks I'm stalking him. That's funny."

She shot me an angry look. "Stay away!" she snapped, and then went back to getting dressed.

I kept an incredulous smile glued to my lips until Amanda and her crew exited the locker room. That's when I finally allowed myself to breathe. Humiliation.

Chapter
Six

The rest of the school day was a nightmare. Not only did I have a pop quiz in Economics, I also had to go through the day making sure I didn't run into Amanda or Dirk again. That would have been too embarrassing.

Back to that pop quiz . . .

And now a multipart extra credit problem:

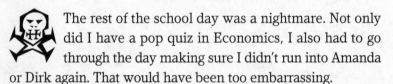

Question: *If teacher A decides to give a short test that nobody in the class sees coming, then whether students B thru Z know the answers or not—and they probably don't, because why would they?—the students still must write some gibberish on a single sheet of loose-leaf paper and turn it in. Now, if there are twenty-six kids in teacher A's class, and there are teacher As in every school in America, and if these teachers give just ten pop quizzes a day, destroying trees by the billions, how long will it take before the ozone layer is totally depleted and the Earth turns into a flaming ball of fire?*

Answer: *YESTERDAY!*

There is no way I could be expected to do well on a pop quiz with all that was going on in my life. Fortunately, Economics was last period. At least I could hide in class until I figured out my next move.

I came up with the perfect plan. I would hole up in the first-floor bathroom until I was sure most of the students were gone for the day. Then I'd sneak to my locker.

When I arrived in the locker area there were just a few students milling about. No one I knew—good. I peeked around each corner carefully, making sure I wasn't about to get ambushed by Dirk or Amanda. Confident they were both gone, I approached my locker and was surprised to see a tiny envelope taped to the front. *Oh, no!* I thought. I couldn't imagine what was in the envelope, but I was certain it wasn't good.

"Open it," a voice called from behind.

"Whaaa!" I nearly jumped out of my skin. I wheeled around to find a smiling Baron Chomsky standing behind me.

"What are you doing here?"

"I'm trying to figure out who left that mysterious note on your locker," he answered with a sly grin.

"We both know who left the note, Baron. You did."

"I'm not saying it wasn't me, but I'm not saying it was me, either."

His cryptic statement was accompanied by an equally cryptic smile. My mind began to reel. *Maybe Amanda was lying about Dirk being her boyfriend. Maybe Dirk does want to go out with me. And maybe this is his way of inviting me to the carnival.*

I yanked the note from my locker and read it.

Join me at the carnival tonight.

There was nothing else. I turned it over and over looking for a signature or some clue as to who it might be from. Could it be true? Did Dirk actually want me to join him at the carnival? My spirits soared.

"Well," Baron said after a few moments. "There's going to be a full moon tonight. Perfect for smooching."

My spirits crashed and burned.

"So it *was* you," I said, releasing the last shred of hope that the note had come from Dirk.

"Of course it was me. Who loves ya, baby?"

"Go away!" The words crept from my lips. I was too upset to scream. I honestly didn't know what I was feeling: anger, pain, embarrassment. My emotions were knotted up inside me.

"But . . ." Baron started to protest, but when he looked in my eyes he stopped cold. "Okay. Maybe we'll do something another time," he said softly. Then he walked away. I was surprised to see him go. It wasn't Baron's style to give up so easily.

It took several moments to realize what he'd seen in my eyes—what had sent him away were tears. I was crying.

I didn't know how long I was seated in the stairwell with my head in my hands when I heard him behind me. I knew he'd come back.

"Look, Baron, I'm . . ." I turned to discover not Baron but Sybil standing behind me. Sybil, sweet Sybil, my best friend, Sybil. She was a sight for sore eyes . . . and trust me, my eyes were pretty sore from all the crying.

"Hi," she said softly.

"Hi yourself."

She was listening to her iPod, her head bopping to the beat as she pretended not to notice the tears on my cheeks.

"What are you still doing here?" My voice was a scant whisper.

"I knew you needed something to get you out of your funk. So . . ." She removed her earbuds and placed them in my ears. "I remembered what always cheers us up no matter what. Tom Jones music."

The opening strains of "It's Not Unusual" filled my ears.

Sybil was right. Whenever we were in the dumps we'd put on one of her grandmother's corny Tom Jones tunes. They always seemed to do the trick. This was our favorite, but today even Tom Jones couldn't ease me out of my funk. I snatched the earbuds from my ears.

"Sorry, Syb. I can't do this right now." I handed her back the buds and told her what had happened. She sat down and gave me a long, comforting hug. "I can't believe we're so out of the loop we had no idea Amanda and Dirk were dating," I said. "We're pathetic. And why would Dirk say maybe if he was already dating Amanda, anyway?"

"You know how boys are. He probably didn't want to say no to my face."

"Why not? He wasn't saying it to *my* face. That was the whole point of *you* asking him."

She changed the subject. "I can't believe Amanda is still holding on to the summer camp thing."

I swallowed hard.

The summer camp thing happened between seventh and eighth grade. This was before Sybil's family had moved to town. Back then, Amanda, Jen and Brandi Paxton (twins), and I were all friends. We did everything together: studied, had sleepovers, went to each other's parties.

During the summer after the seventh grade, while we were all away at summer camp, I came down with the chicken pox.

When I was diagnosed, the counselors immediately sent me home so that I wouldn't give it to any of the other girls. At home, I spent an entire, miserable summer in the house, away from my three friends.

I healed over the summer, and by the time school started in the fall, I was no longer under quarantine. That's when the real misery began. Something had changed between me and my friends over the summer, something I knew nothing about. I couldn't wait to see them, but on the first day of school Amanda and the girls gave me the silent treatment. At first I thought it was a joke.

"Come on, guys. Enough!" I said during lunch. Not one of them looked at me or responded. They just moved away.

For days after, I racked my brain trying to figure out what I could have done to deserve this. I tried calling each of them to find out, but they wouldn't take my calls. I told myself not to panic: *This kind of snubbing happens in middle school all the time.* I figured I'd wait it out. I knew that eventually the snubbed friends usually made up with each other and things got back to normal. But by Halloween I realized that wasn't going to happen with us.

I lay in bed at night in tears over the loss of my best friends. *What could I have done that was so wrong?*

By the end of eighth grade, Jen and Brandi had moved away. It was the perfect time to ask Amanda what I had done to deserve the snub. But by then she had the Twigettes, and I had joined the ranks of those who were derided or laughed at.

It had happened a long time ago, but the thought of it in that moment stung as if it was happening right then. I buried the pain back deep inside, where it had lived for so long.

"Forget about Amanda, and Baron . . . *and* Dirk," said Sybil. "We always have a good time together. We don't need them.

All we need is you, me, and Tom Jones. Hey, maybe we'll even meet boyfriends at the carnival. That'll show them."

I stiffened. "What are you talking about?"

"Us going to the carnival, of course."

"Let me see if I'm getting this right. Since I can't go to the carnival with the most gorgeous boy at school, it sounds like you're suggesting that you and I should be dateless freaks and go to the carnival *alone*."

"Well . . ."

"How does that solve anything?"

"It's better than going with Baron Chomsky," she charged.

"No, it isn't. It's the same thing!"

She winced when I compared her to Baron.

"Well, you were going to the carnival with me and Dirk. It's just one less person."

"No. I was going to the carnival with Dirk alone. Me and Dirk. No you."

"Oh."

There was something not right with that *oh*. It had an odd, distant quality to it. "What, Sybil?"

"Nothing."

I tried looking her in the eye, but she wouldn't let me. "You did ask Dirk to go to the carnival with *me*, right?"

"Well . . ."

"Sybil!"

Words tumbled out of her. "I was going to, but the truth is I want to go out with Dirk as badly as you do, and since I was the one doing the asking, I didn't think it would hurt to ask him to go with both of us."

My temperature began to rise. "Your Dirk Conrad was supposed to be a benchmark!"

"I know. But I really like the benchmark."

"Then why was *I* the one who was supposed to talk to him on the phone last night if we're *both* going to the carnival with him?"

"You know how shy I am around boys." She was babbling away, not making any sense. Then all of a sudden the pieces began falling into place.

"Wait a minute! No wonder you had Dirk's daily schedule. You've been scouting Dirk for yourself all along, haven't you?"

Her eyes dipped to the floor. "Well . . . I figured it would be easier for him to accept our offer if it wasn't an official date. And everyone would see him with you *and* me, and nobody would be able to tell whose boyfriend he was. Of course he wouldn't be anyone's boyfriend, but nobody would know that. . . . It would be a win-win. We could both claim him. And who knows, maybe by the end of the night he'd choose one of us. . . ." More words spouted from her like a leaky faucet. I stared at her in disbelief. Sybil really *was* from another planet. No Earth person in their right mind would think her plan made any sense.

"Going to the carnival with you and Dirk wouldn't be fun, Syb. It would be *embarrassing.*"

Sybil's head snapped back as if she'd been punched in the jaw. I could see the pain on her face and should have stopped there, but part of me was glad she was feeling pain, especially after what she'd done. I went in for the kill. "What kind of *idiot* can't see that Dirk showing up at the carnival with both of us is the ultimate embarrassment? That's a pity date!"

"Did you just call me an idiot?" she said. "At least I'm not spazzing out over somebody else's boyfriend. *That's* idiotic!"

"Oh, really? No wonder he went running into Amanda Culpepper's arms. He was probably trying to get away from the stalker—you!"

We sat in the stairwell tossing words at each other like hand grenades.

Then finally she said, "Forget you, Margot. If you don't want to cheer yourself up and have some fun, I'll just go to the carnival without you."

"Go ahead. I'm sure you and *Tom Jones* will have a ball on your *pity date*."

"We will!" she said.

"Good!" I said.

"Later, hater." She snapped her earbuds back into place and stormed off.

I watched her go. I'm sure if I had called out she would have come back, but I didn't. I couldn't. I again looked at the invitation Baron had left on my locker. I read aloud: "Join me at the carnival tonight." I ripped it to shreds.

Chapter
Seven

 My walk to school alone the next morning was rather peaceful. A freak thunderstorm had hit the city the previous night, complete with sheets of pelting rain that left the morning air crisp and fragrant.

I arrived at school and went right to my locker. There was no Sybil standing there smiling at me like a maniac. How one person could be so cheerful in the morning had always annoyed me. Mornings were miserable—didn't she know that? I smiled. Life without Sybil was turning out to be quite excellent.

"Margot!" Sybil's voice rang out. It hit me like nails on a chalkboard.

I turned. Sybil was standing near the stairwell surrounded by a group of grungy-looking girls. *Wait a minute. Aren't those Amanda's Twigettes? Why are their clothes all gunked up? And what could they possibly be doing with Sybil?*

"Margot!" she called again.

Then it dawned on me. She'd hooked up with the it-girls at the carnival last night. She's blond and skinny. She'd been accepted into the Twigette sorority and was rubbing it in.

"I don't have time for you, Sybil Mulcahy," I called back. "And I can't imagine why anyone would." I added this last part for the benefit of the Twigettes. They needed to know their new friend wasn't even popular with me.

Hearing my voice, the girls surrounding Sybil stopped what they were doing and slowly turned toward me.

Oh, my goodness. Who did their makeup this morning?

The girls' skin was all green and crumbly, as if they'd gotten makeup tips from the Munsters. *Wait a minute. Is that some hip, new fashion thing I don't know about?* Amanda and her crew were always on top of the latest makeup and fashion tips. I was suddenly envious of their hideous green complexions.

The moment the girls turned away from Sybil she shoved past them and raced over to me. "Zombies!" she squawked. "Come." Before I could respond she grabbed my hand, yanking me down the hall and into the first-floor girls' bathroom.

"What is the matter with you?" I demanded as she slammed the bathroom door and leaned against it.

"Z-zombies," she stammered again. A low, rhythmic moaning began on the other side of the door.

"Zazombie? Is that what you call that green makeup your new friends are wearing? I think it looks ridiculous. Um . . . where did they get it?"

Outside the moaning grew louder, as bodies began slamming into the door.

"No!" Sybil grabbed my shoulders. "Listen to me . . ."

Sybil launched into an incredible tale: "I went to the carnival last night. Most of the kids from our school were there." Her voice dropped an octave. "I was alone and not having any fun, watching everyone enjoying themselves. So, I decided to leave and got home just before the storm hit. I'm sorry we fought, Margot. I miss you," she said.

I still wasn't ready to forgive her. "Get back to your story."

She took a deep breath. "This morning I came to school early because I didn't want to run into you walking, and when I got here everyone was a zombie."

"That is the most ridiculous thing I've ever heard. There's no such thing as zombies. You've been watching too many horror flicks."

Just then, the doorknob to the bathroom turned.

"Ahhh!" Sybil screamed as she skittered away from the door, retreating to the far wall across the room. As she cowered in the corner, the door began to open.

Chapter
Eight

 Slowly they entered. There were three of them, their movements stiff and plodding. I looked into each of their eyes and saw emptiness. Still, I couldn't believe the Twigettes had become zombies. There had to be a logical explanation for why they were acting so strange. They started toward me.

"Hello, ladies. I see we're into the grunge look today." I was going for the cheery approach.

They must have still been in the clothes they'd worn to the carnival the previous night. Their outfits were casual-chic, but ripped in spots and smeared with dirt.

"Mmmmmmmm," the girls were moaning. It was a low-pitched, eerie sound filled with despair, which started deep in their chests and rumbled up their throats.

I took a step back.

"I guess you guys will want to fix your makeup now. I'll just get out of your way. And I must say you really could use a touch-up this morning—no offense."

"Mmmmmmmm," they moaned. I stepped farther into the

room, away from the sinks and mirrors. They ignored the sinks and mirrors and continued toward me.

"Okay, no touch-up. That's cool. Actually, I kinda like the green and crumbly thing. Retro." I was nearing the wall, practically on top of Sybil. The zombies closed in on us.

"Stay back," Sybil called. "If they bite you, you'll join them among the living dead."

"Nobody wants to bite anybody. Besides, either you're dead or alive, you can't be *living* and *dead*." I looked over at the girls again. Their mouths had parted, and hungry spittle drizzled from their teeth. "Um . . . okay, scratch what I just said about biting."

Just then the bathroom door opened again, and Amanda Culpepper entered. At least it looked like Amanda Culpepper. But this Amanda was wearing a rumpled yellow sundress, and she was green like the others.

"Oh my," I whispered, panic rising inside me. "Amanda Culpepper is . . . a zombie."

"*Now* you believe me?" Sybil stammered.

"Yes," I said, as the magnitude of the situation became clear. "There's really no other explanation. The Amanda Culpepper I know would never use the first-floor girls' bathroom."

For a girl, using the bathrooms at Salesian could be a tricky proposition if she didn't know the rules. The third-floor girls' bathroom by the science labs was for the coolest of cool girls. If you weren't cool, you'd better have a deadly stomach virus to enter. On the opposite end of the spectrum, the first-floor girls' bathroom by the entrance was for freshmen, freaks, and geeks. Any upperclassman entering the freaks' domain—even if she were near death—would be committing social suicide. Amanda would never, ever come in here.

While the other girls moaned, the Amanda thing snarled loudly as she started toward us.

My back was now against the wall, as was Sybil's. "They're going to bite us; they're going to bite us!" Sybil was losing it.

"*Growwwl!*" the Amanda thing said loudly. She pushed her way to the front of the pack.

"Oh, my goodness! She's the leader. She wants us for herself," Sybil called, screwing her back into the wall, covering her face with her arms.

The Amanda thing began snarling orders to the others. Slowly they turned and shuffled from the room. Then she stepped toward us.

"Don't you come any closer, Amanda." I struck a fake karate pose.

I don't know anything about karate. I'd seen the stance in a movie somewhere.

"Hi-yaaaa!" I screamed as I whipped my hands through the air, hoping Amanda might have second thoughts about attacking a ninja.

I looked into the Amanda thing's eyes, and through her snarling, I could swear she was laughing at me. She slogged to a halt, flipped her nose into the air, then turned and began shuffling after the others. Stopping at the door, she threw one last haughty snarl into the air and exited. Sybil and I were alone.

"That was close," she said with a sigh. "You saved us."

"No, I didn't. She wasn't afraid of me."

"Of course she was."

I shook my head. "I'm not good enough," I said softly. Sybil stared at me. "Don't you see? She didn't want us for herself. She barely acknowledged us. She only came in here to make sure her friends didn't bite me. And you want to know why? Because *I'm* not good enough!" I was suddenly livid.

"B-but they're zombies."

"I know. It's the ultimate insult. Not good enough to become a zombie."

Sybil's eyes widened. "Are you saying you *want* to become a zombie?"

"Of course not. But I am sick and tired of being snubbed."

She shook her head briefly before saying, "Whatever you say, Margot. But now we have to get out of here."

She was right. We needed to tell the authorities what was going on at Salesian. That meant getting out of the building and away from campus. We calmed ourselves as best we could, and ventured cautiously into the corridor.

Chapter
Nine

 I could hardly believe my eyes. The place was crawling with zombies. *Zombies.* It was a ridiculous thing to imagine, something out of a horror flick, and yet it seemed to be true.

"There's so many of them," Sybil whispered.

It was then I noticed the zombies moving sluggishly through the halls were still among their normal circle of friends: popular zombies, Goth zombies, nerd zombies, all roaming in their close-knit groups.

"They're still hanging in their cliques," I said.

"I can see that." There was a hint of outrage in Sybil's voice. "Being a zombie hasn't changed anything around here."

"I guess not."

Isolated screams erupted from all parts of the building as the remaining living students were set upon by the zombies. I saw a lone student in the stairwell under attack by stoner nerd zombies. We passed a classroom where a teacher was struggling on the floor beneath a horde of loser zombies. I surmised that after you were attacked by a clique, you became a card-carrying member of that clique.

I glanced at Sybil. Fear was once again rising in her eyes. "They're turning everyone into zombies," she said.

"Not us. We just need to stay together and stick with the plan," I whispered. "Act like them." I began walking like a zombie toward the south exit.

"Where are you going?" Sybil called. Her voice rang out in the corridor.

Slowly the zombies turned their attention to her.

"Stop talking! Moan, zombie walk, and follow me," I whispered out of the corner of my mouth.

Sybil stared at me with a faraway look in her eyes. My words weren't making any sense to her. Her sanity was slipping away. More zombies emerged from their catatonic state and began slowly advancing on her.

"Oh, my!" She gasped.

"Don't panic. Put a vacant stare on your face and zombie walk."

The zombies were getting closer.

I continued zombie walking toward the exit door as a pack of nerd zombies advanced on Sybil. *I have to let her go*, I thought. *There is no way I'm going to let them turn me into a nerd.*

Visions of Amanda snubbing me in the bathroom flashed through my mind. *The nerve of her!* She didn't want the Twigettes to bite me because I would have become an it-girl zombie. Even as a zombie, she couldn't stand for that to happen. I made up my mind right then that if the it-girls didn't bite me, there was no way I was settling for a bite from a lesser zombie.

I continued putting distance between myself, Sybil, and

the zombies. I glanced back and saw her frozen to the spot, practically surrounded by snarling, moaning zombies—Goth zombies, loser zombies.

Uh-uh! No way! I do not want to become a Goth—although, black is slimming.

Yet as peeved as I was with Sybil over the Dirk thing, I knew I couldn't just walk away. We'd come too far together for me to do that.

"Oh, all right!" I said with a sigh.

Stiffly, I walked back toward the pack of zombies that surrounded her. I pushed past an emo zombie, took Sybil's hand, and yanked her along.

"You do not want that emo to bite you. You hate that kind of music." Sybil nodded. I didn't know if I was getting through to her, but she allowed me to pull her along. The zombies followed. "Zombie walk, Sybil. It's our only chance."

That seemed to snap her out of her fog, and she began walking stiffly beside me, shuffling her feet. She glanced back over her shoulder. "They're still following us."

"That's because you're not acting like a zombie. Put a vacant stare on your face, as if someone just told a joke and you have no idea what they're talking about."

Her face contorted. "Is this vacant enough?"

"No, you look annoyed."

More zombies joined the group following us. They seemed to be coming from everywhere.

"Think back to chemistry class. Remember the look on my face the first time I saw the periodic table of elements?"

Sybil thought for a moment, then her face went blank. "Like this?"

"Yes, exactly! Now just keep walking. . . . Not too fast." A part of me wanted to run. But how far would we get? Zombies were coming at us from every direction. Our only chance was to fool them into believing we were zombies like them. If that didn't work, we were about to join the living dead.

Just then the PA system squawked.

"Hellooo, and a fabulous Friday morning to the Knights of Salesian High." Principal Taft's morning announcement echoed throughout the school.

The zombies around us all stopped as if they were listening. Sybil and I were forgotten. We reached the exit door.

"They're not going to attack," Sybil said. She stood stone-still, keeping her face expressionless, and spoke softly. "We need to zombie walk out of here and right to the police station."

"Not yet. I'm not going anywhere until I find out why Principal Taft is normal like us. Maybe he knows something." I started zombie walking away from the exit. "You coming?"

"Where?" Her voice was filled with trepidation.

"To Principal Taft's office. There's someone in this school who doesn't seem to be afraid of the zombies, and I'd like to know why."

Chapter

Ten

Principal Taft's office was near the main entrance on the first floor. To get there you had to pass through the general office where teachers came in the mornings to punch in and students went to sort out daily problems. Inside the general office, behind a wooden door that was always closed, was Taft's office.

As Principal Taft went on with the announcement, Sybil and I walked slowly down to the general office, opened the door, and let ourselves in. The office was empty. No teachers, no students, no half-eaten bodies, no zombies. We could hear Principal Taft's voice coming from the other side of his door. I tried to open it. Locked. I knocked. No response.

Principal Taft continued his morning announcement as if we weren't there.

"Why doesn't he answer?" Sybil asked.

Without responding, I knocked louder. "Principal Taft. It's Margot Johnson and Sybil Mulcahy. We need to talk."

Silence for a moment, then his voice rang out: "Good

morning, ladies. And what a fantastic Friday it is." *You could say that again*, I thought. "What can I do for you?"

"You can start by letting us in," I called. There was another long silence. "Principal Taft? Are you there?"

"Yes, yes. But I'm afraid I can't do that. Perhaps you should go see your guidance counselor, Miss Everheart."

That would never do. If Miss Everheart had gone to her office this morning, by now she was a zombie.

"Principal Taft, we really need to talk to *you*."

"Well . . . then come back after eighth period. Maybe I can squeeze you in then."

A low moaning began just beyond the general office door. The zombies in the corridor outside had heard our voices. Pretty soon they'd be trying to get in.

"Um . . . I guess we should come back," Sybil whispered as she fearfully eyed the outer door.

"We're not coming back. Who knows if we'll even be able to come back. Principal Taft!" I hollered. "I want to know why you're not dead or a zombie! And I want to know now!" More silence. And then the lock on his office door clicked open.

"Come in."

Principal Harvey Taft was a large, round man with almond-colored skin and a hearty laugh. Normally he was the picture of authority. So imagine my surprise when we entered his office and found him standing on his desk. His jacket was off, draped over the back of his chair, and sweat stains were beginning to show through his once-crisp white shirt.

"I hope you girls have a hall pass," he said, trying to sound authoritative.

"Principal Taft, why are you on your desk?" Sybil asked.

"I, uhh, thought I saw, um, a mouse."

"You're afraid of mice?"

"No. Of course not," he said, grasping for a sense of dignity. "I . . . thought I saw a mouse on my desk, and . . . I was trying to step on it."

And these are our role models. Pathetic.

"Zombies," I said. Nothing more. I looked up at him and waited.

"Zombies? I haven't seen any zombies."

But I hadn't asked if he'd seen any zombies—so obviously he had.

"Principal Taft, we need for you to tell us the truth. And if we don't get answers from you, we're going home and telling our parents." I stared at him for a long moment, the challenge hanging in the air. He didn't move.

"Okay, Syb, let's go. Our parents will be very interested to hear there's a crisis at school and Principal Taft isn't doing anything about it." I turned and started for the door.

"Wait," he called.

I turned back. Principal Taft reached into his breast pocket, pulled something out, and threw it on the floor in front of us. It was a sliver of raw meat.

"Eww!" Sybil cried. "Gross."

Principal Taft sighed. "Phew! You're not one of them. I had to make sure." There was relief in his words as he got down off his desk and collapsed into his chair. Just then the bell for first period rang.

"Don't try and get rid of us by telling us to go to class," I warned. "We want to know what you know." I stared at him long and hard.

"You're right. I shouldn't have pretended everything was hunky-dory. It's not." His shoulders slumped forward. "I'm going to need your help on this, young ladies."

The change in him caught me off guard. "Sure," I said.

"How can we help?" asked Sybil.

"Here, sit," he said, gesturing toward two chairs.

"I went to the carnival last night," he said, after we were seated. "It was a glorious evening. The student body and faculty were all present, and everyone was having a wonderful time. Out of nowhere, dark clouds rolled in, filling the sky." His voice turned ominous.

"It was then I noticed some of the boys were becoming a bit surly. As the storm hit, more students began acting aggressively. I conferred with the carnival officials and decided to call an end to the evening. After that I left. But as I drove away I observed a change in all the students present. Their gaits had become slow and plodding, and their eyes were blank, as if they were sleepwalking."

"It happened at the carnival last night," I said. I turned to Sybil. "That's why you and I are still normal. You left early and I never went."

"We have to contact the authorities about this," Sybil said. She reached for the phone.

"No, no. We shouldn't do that." Worry lines appeared on Taft's brow.

"But we need to do something," she said.

"Don't you see? They'll blame me. I was the major authority figure present." He beseeched us with his eyes.

"Just tell them the truth like you told us," said Sybil.

"I suppose I could," he said. "But I have a better idea. We continue as if nothing's happened."

We both stared at him.

"How is that better?" I asked. I couldn't believe what he was saying. He wanted us to ignore the fact that our classmates had all become zombies.

"I've been watching them," he said. "I know what they like

and don't like. I know what they fear. We could easily coexist with them if we wanted to."

"But why would we want to?" I could feel myself slowly losing it. He was asking us to take our lives into our hands and try to coexist with zombies.

"For me." There was a near pleading in the words.

I could tell that Sybil was feeling sympathy for him. But all of our classmates had turned into monsters. We at least needed to find out if we could turn them back.

I looked at Taft and shook my head. "I don't know, Principal Taft."

Desperation sprang into his voice. "I've been a high school principal for a long time—too long, in fact. And finally I'm less than a semester away from a promotion to district supervisor, and *this* happens. I deserve better." He put his head in his hands and wagged it sadly. Sybil and I looked at each other again.

"So we should just pretend this hasn't happened?" I asked.

"No, I'm not saying that at all." He lifted his head. "But would it be so bad if we did? Just until the end of the semester. There's only seven weeks left. That's practically no time at all."

"I know, sir. But the authorities need to know about this," I insisted.

"You know if we go to the police they'll blame me. Is that fair? Just allow me seven weeks to try and fix it." He stood and put his hands together as if in prayer. "Please!"

I was beginning to feel sorry for him, too. "Even if we wanted to keep this a secret, sir, somebody will find out."

"Maybe. But I don't think so. The students came to school this morning like they've been doing all semester, and right now I bet they're headed for first-period class."

"Why would zombies go to class?" asked Sybil.

"Sense memory, I suppose. They're doing what they've always done. And they'll keep doing it every day until the end of the semester . . . or until I can fix things."

I thought back to when Sybil and I zombie walked toward the building's south exit, surrounded by moaning zombies. As soon as the morning announcement began, the zombies had all stopped and listened as they did every morning. We were forgotten.

"What about parents?" Sybil asked.

"Parents already think you kids are from another planet. They'll look at this new behavior as a phase. And the few parents who push the issue will join the living dead. So they won't be complaining."

It seemed Principal Taft had thought of everything. Still, I knew what he was proposing was wrong. "I'm sorry, Principal Taft, but—"

"Margot Jean Johnson, how would you like to be president of the Homecoming Committee?" he suddenly said. The odd request caught me off guard.

"Amanda Culpepper is homecoming president," I said.

"Amanda Culpepper is a zombie." A sly look crossed his face. "I'm going to pass a rule right now that no zombie can be in charge of anything at Salesian High."

And suddenly, what had seemed so wrong a few moments before was starting to seem right. Why should Amanda get to run everything? *Serves her right for not biting me. And for ostracizing me in the eighth grade.*

"What about the Prom Committee?" I heard myself asking.

"That's usually reserved for seniors, but seeing as how you're willing to help me out with my little problem, you are now chairman of the Prom Committee. And we can have any prom theme you wish."

"Prom queen?"

"I know of only two candidates, and they're both standing right in front of me. I think you're a shoo-in." He winked at me.

Suddenly my thoughts were consumed with all the accolades I'd been denied for as far back as I could remember.

"Yearbook Committee?"

"Yours."

"Head cheerleader?"

"You."

"Captain of the debate team?"

"Yes!"

"Wait. I don't want that. That's social suicide. I was just testing you." My high school manifesto flashed through my mind. Here was my opportunity to have the best semester of my life. And all I had to do was go along with his . . . ridiculous plan.

"Lunchroom monitor," Sybil suddenly said. We both turned and stared at her.

"You want to be a lunchroom monitor?" My words were filled with disbelief.

"Yes."

"A lunch . . . room . . . monitor?" I said the words slowly—not for her benefit. I wanted to make sure I was hearing myself correctly.

"I know it sounds silly, but I've always wanted to be a lunchroom monitor."

"Not only are you a lunchroom monitor, young lady, but you're the *head* lunchroom monitor," Principal Taft said.

"I get to run the cafeteria? Yes!" Sybil said, pumping her fist.

I didn't ask why she wanted the ridiculous position. At the moment I didn't care. The pendulum of popularity was swinging in my direction. My dreams were coming true.

The air of gloom that had surrounded Principal Taft a few moments earlier lifted. He smiled at us, a sly twinkle in his eye. "So, ladies, do we have a deal?"

I faced Sybil. "The principal of our school is asking for our help."

"I know."

"We'd be horrible student citizens if we turned him down."

"I know."

"So, we'll just have to suck it up, and take over all those tasks that used to belong to Amanda Culpepper."

"I know!"

I was finding it hard to contain the laughter bubbling up inside of me. I couldn't believe our luck.

"A good student citizen should be able to get along with any visitor to our school, even a zombie," Principal Taft said, sounding like a principal again. "I'm going to give you my six rules for living successfully among zombies."

I pulled out a pen and paper and wrote them down:

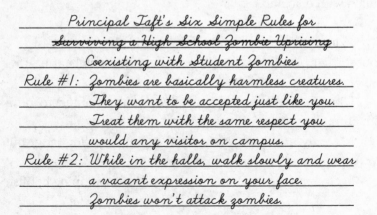

Principal Taft's ~~Six Simple Rules for~~ ~~Surviving a High School Zombie Uprising~~ Coexisting with Student Zombies

Rule #1: Zombies are basically harmless creatures. They want to be accepted just like you. Treat them with the same respect you would any visitor on campus.

Rule #2: While in the halls, walk slowly and wear a vacant expression on your face. Zombies won't attack zombies.

Rule #3: Never travel alone. Move in packs. Follow the crowd. Zombies detest blatant displays of individuality.

*Rule #4: In class, sit quietly in your seats and wait to be called upon. **Do not** raise your hands or make any sudden moves. No one hates a know-it-all more than a zombie.*

Rule #5: If a zombie should attack, do not run. Instead, throw raw steak at him. Zombies love raw meat. This display of kindness will go a long way.

Rule #6: Wear a vial filled with fish oil around your neck at all times. Zombies detest the smell of fish. This is your way of saying "Hey, Mister Zombie, respect my space." If students and zombies respect each other's space, our school will be a very happy place.

When I finished writing, Taft pulled out a Baggie. It contained hunks of raw steak. "You need to carry Baggies filled with meat slivers with you at all times," he said.

"Gross," said Sybil, turning up her nose at the raw meat.

"Does it have to be steak?" I asked.

"I don't know. Why?"

"We're more of a hamburger family."

"Any raw meat should work, but if hamburger doesn't work, or if you ever find yourselves in close quarters with a zombie for any reason, a sharp rap on the nose with a rolled-up newspaper should stun them long enough to get you out of the tight spot."

And that was it. That's all he'd been able to figure out so far.

That tiny bit of information was all we had to keep ourselves alive for the next seven weeks, until the end of the semester.

On the bright side, I was being given the opportunity to live out my dream and realize my manifesto. I'd always wanted to be an it-girl, but the Amanda Culpeppers of the world were always standing in my way. But no more. If I went along with Principal Taft's plan, my junior year would be exactly what I'd always dreamed it should be. And all I had to do to enjoy it was stay alive.

"What a crazy day," Sybil said with a sigh. Sybil and I had been out of school several hours and were in my bedroom. When she spoke I realized we'd been there for quite some time and neither of us had said anything. That was unusual. Normally when Sybil and I were in my room we were buzzing with chatter.

For my part, I'd been distracted ever since our meeting with Principal Taft. Something inside me was different. I knew I was excited over the prospect of living out my manifesto, but something else was going on. It was as if a door had opened inside me, and something dark within my soul had stepped through it.

"Very crazy," I replied.

"Margot, I'm sorry for not telling you I asked Dirk to go to the carnival with both of us. It was deceitful."

"If I'd gone to the carnival with Dirk I'd probably be a zombie now." My voice was somber. The thought had been on my mind for a while. Our argument had saved my life.

"I know. I saw him this morning in a pack of jock zombies

patrolling the corridor." Her voice lowered. "Margot, I need to know we're still friends."

"Of course we're friends. Best friends. Friends have fights."

"Not us."

A smile blossomed on my lips. "I guess we can't say that anymore. Can we?"

"Guess not," she replied, returning the smile. And just like that, all was forgiven.

Despite the perk of being head lunchroom monitor—which I didn't see as a perk at all—Sybil still felt we needed to help our fellow classmates. I no longer shared the sentiment.

"What can we do for them? They're zombies." I was surprised I felt no pity. "Besides, I'm sure Principal Taft is doing all he can to find out what happened."

"But maybe we can help, too. Maybe we can find a way to change them back ourselves."

I stared at her. I was trying to come up with a reason why I'd want to change them back. I couldn't come up with one. Some of those kids had been nothing but pains in the butt my entire time in high school. They were the ones who'd made my two years and two months at Salesian so miserable, with all their little cliques constantly reminding me of what an outsider I was. I didn't say it out loud, but I was actually happy I didn't have to deal with them anymore.

"What can we do?" I repeated. I knew what I wanted to do—nothing.

"We can go to the carnival and look for clues to find out what happened to them," Sybil said.

Leave it to *nice* Sybil to come up with a logical answer to my question. She clearly lacked the mean gene.

"But suppose we run into zombies at the carnival?"

"We'll bring raw meat and wear fish oil. And we already

know how to act. Come on, Margot. You know it's the right thing to do."

So what if it is? I thought. *I don't want to change them back. I want to be on the Homecoming Committee and the Prom Committee. I want to be prom queen!*

The conversation was putting me in a really bad mood. I should be spending my evening thinking up themes for the homecoming celebration, not how to help my classmates out of their little zombie problem. Didn't I have my own problems? Like should the new cheerleader outfits be royal blue or teal?

Just then a brilliant idea hit me. It was as if a lightbulb had actually clicked on above my head. I would go to the carnival with Sybil not to look for answers, but to keep her from finding any. If we didn't find anything, I was guaranteed our classmates would remain zombies forever—or at least until the end of the semester.

"Sybil, you're right. We should go to the carnival and look for clues that might help us change our classmates back to normal," I said with fake sincerity.

"Thank you, Margot. I knew you'd come around," she replied.

The dark thing inside me smiled.

The carnival was set up on a vacant lot at the edge of the industrial part of town. There were several rides: a Ferris wheel, Tilt-a-Whirl, and the Hammer, along with an assortment of gaming booths where people tried their hand at tossing rings over pegs, knocking over milk bottles, and bursting balloons with water pistols.

We arrived at the carnival site just after 8 P.M. to discover the carnival was gone. No tents, no rides, no booths, nothing.

The area that just last night had been lit up by hundreds of multicolored lights and teeming with excited teenagers roaming the midway was now a desolate wasteland.

"It's gone," Sybil said as we surveyed the empty lot.

"I can see that."

"But how? Nobody said last night was the *last night*."

"But apparently it was." With the crisis averted my mind began to shift. "You know, I've been thinking about the new cheerleader outfits," I said. "Belly shirts are so passé."

"Not now, Margot. We have to find out what happened out here last night."

Sybil's niceness was starting to get on my nerves. I thought of all the causes she had taken up since I'd known her: Save the Bay, Save the Seals, Save the Whales. Now it was . . . Save the Zombies.

"How?" I barked. "The carnival is gone. There's nothing to see, no one to talk to. We should thank our lucky stars there aren't any zombies hanging around." Fumes from the icky vials of fish oil we'd hung around our necks wafted up my nose. It did nothing to brighten my mood.

"We need to search the area," Sybil said, rummaging in her purse.

"It's dark out. We can hardly see our hands in front of our faces."

"I have my lucky flashlight."

"Oh. Right."

I'd given her a set of exercise DVDs for her birthday. The tiny key chain penlight was a premium that came with the gift.

"It's perfect!" she had said when she opened the gift and saw the penlight. Turns out she'd dropped an earring under her bed getting ready for the party. We went right to her bedroom and used the penlight to find it. When we did her face lit up: "Oh, Margot, you always know the perfect thing to get me."

I secretly cursed that penlight: *Who needs a flashlight to exercise? Stupid premium.*

She pulled the tiny penlight from her purse and began searching the dirty, filthy, smelly lot, digging through soil and refuse. Then an even more putrid stench hit me. "Ew! Something smells like stinky tennis shoes covered with cheese and then left out in the rain."

I knew that particular stink very well thanks to my cheesy little brother.

"What are we looking for, anyway?" I grumbled, pinching my nose to shut out the repugnant odor.

"I don't know. Something . . . relevant."

"Let's see. Ooh, there's a corn dog stick. Is that relevant? Or maybe that mysterious soft drink cup is just what we need to save our classmates." Sarcasm flowed from my lips. "Or how about that rock? Yes, that's it! The magic zombie rock. Sybil, I do believe we found just what—"

Crunch!

Both our heads whipped around as we stared in the direction of the sound. Blackness greeted our eyes.

"What was that?" Sybil whispered.

"Zombies," I whispered back.

My heart was pounding. Every ounce of me wanted to run, but I stood by as Sybil aimed the tiny beam in the direction of the sound. Nothing. Whatever we had heard—*crunch, crunch*—was moving. The tiny beam of the light now slid shakily across the lot in the direction of the moving sound.

"It's time to go," I said, my voice quaking. I yanked on her sleeve.

And then the flashlight's beam discovered the thing moving in the shadows. *"Ahhh!"* we both screamed as the black cat zipped away into the darkness.

"See. Heh-heh. It was just a cat," Sybil said, trying to laugh it off.

"Yeah," I replied. "Heh-heh. A cat." But I knew we were both thinking that the sound we'd first heard couldn't have been a cat. It was most definitely the sound of human, or *inhuman*, footsteps. Someone or *something* had been watching us.

Later that night, I sat alone in my room contemplating the future. The darkness lounging in my soul was happy my classmates were all zombies. It told me there was nothing anyone could do about it. *We have to get on with our lives.* It promised me a new life where I was no longer the girl on the sidelines passing the time, observing the good life from the outside instead of living it. I was about to become the queen bee of Salesian High.

It told me to enjoy it.

Zombies are incredibly predictable.

Our first day at school among the living dead started out uneventfully. The zombies came to school and went to the same classes they'd gone to when they were among the living. They lumbered through the halls with a lazy gait, moving on instinct and muscle memory rather than free will or desire. At first, it was frightening moving amongst them with their pasty complexions and mouths twisted into grotesque smiles. But eventually, Sybil and I shook our fears. We moved easily from pack to pack, navigating the corridors of Salesian High.

Don't get me wrong—we could never totally relax around them. They *were* zombies. A sudden move, a joyous laugh, even a raised eyebrow, any expression of individuality, and we could be dead meat—literally. But as long as we remained expressionless and our movements mirrored the pack, we were safe.

Soon going to school amongst the zombies, walking stiffly and staring off dreamily became second nature to us both.

One day while Sybil and I were on the third floor, traveling in a pack of grunge zombies, headed to history class, something out of the ordinary happened. As we passed the science lab some mice escaped, darting from the room and across the corridor. This sudden burst of frenetic energy got the zombies' attention. They seemed to awaken from their dreamlike state. Slowly, they got down on all fours in an attempt to catch and eat the mice.

It was a ridiculous exercise. The herky-jerky movements of the mice dumbfounded the sluggish zombies, who ineptly grasped at the tiny rodents, but wound up with handfuls of air. I glanced over at Sybil. We were the only two in the corridor still standing. She shot me a warning glance, then got down on her hands and knees. I didn't move. The zombies were too preoccupied with the mice to notice me. Sybil's eyes were on me, signaling me to get down.

I shot her a look of exasperation. *Do I have to do everything they do?* I wondered. Suppose I did join them. Heaven forbid I actually caught a mouse in my bare hands. *Yech!* If I didn't scream, I'd faint, and that would be the end of me. So I figured it was better to stand passively, observing the silly exercise, than to get on my hands and knees, which might lead to my demise.

Just then a pack of zombies turned the corner, led by Amanda Culpepper. She looked horrible. Her pasty complexion was accented by a sickly green pallor. Her once cute yellow Bebe sundress was smudged with dirt and frayed around the hem, draping her tiny frame like a rag. I stood silently, hoping she and her friends would move on. No such luck. Their dead, black eyes all moved to me.

Sheesh! The things a girl has to do to be prom queen.

Slowly I got down on the floor, pretending to reach in the direction of the darting mice—*ick, ick, ick!*

Amanda and the it-girl zombies got down on the floor as well, joining the fray. *How embarrassing*, I thought. *The former queen of Salesian High crawling around on her hands and knees, trying to make a meal out of mice. Oh, how the mighty have fallen.*

I thought back to when Amanda ruled the school with her designer wardrobe and movie-star good looks. I remembered the cutting laughter that could send me and others home sobbing, our psyches in shreds. I promised myself as the new queen of Salesian High, I would be different. I would lead with dignity and grace, and never look through a classmate as if she didn't exist just because she didn't look or act like me. I would be a shining example for it-girls across America—once I got up off the floor.

At that moment a mouse darted between two pursuing zombies. The scrambling mouse leaped into the air, and landed in my lap.

"AHHHHHHHHHHHH!"

They say time stops in moments of crisis. I've heard stories of people in horrific car accidents who've said the whole thing played out moment by moment in front of them in slow motion. I never believed any of those stories. I always thought the people who told them were being overly dramatic. I couldn't fathom that something occurring in a split second could play out like a DVD stuck in slo-mo—until it happened to me.

The next several things I am about to tell you happened in a matter of seconds.

Slow Motion

My ear-piercing scream alerted the zombies. Their heads jerkily whipped from side to side as they tried to determine the origin of the sound. Then one by one their eyes all fell on me. Dark eyes.

Ravenous eyes. Their mouths opened, revealing fangs dripping with saliva.

The zombies began crawling in my direction.

I glanced over at Sybil. Terror was frozen onto her face. It seemed at any moment she'd faint dead away.

Thinking more quickly than I ever thought possible, I grabbed at Sybil's hand. "Grrr," I said.

I pulled her hand open, pretending to snatch something from it. Then I cupped my hands to my mouth and began making noisy, gobbling sounds. I pretended to chew, swallow, then glanced around at the leering zombies. I screamed again.

"AHHHHHHHHHHHHH!" But I filled this second scream with the primal delight of a cavewoman who had just discovered fire.

Normal Time

I put my head down and went back to sluggishly swatting at the remaining mice, keeping a watchful eye on the zombies around me, hoping, praying they'd fall for my little charade. Slowly they too went back to the task at hand. A fleeing mouse somehow landed in the hand of one of Amanda's bunch.

"Rrrrrrrrrrrrrrrrr," she croaked, mimicking my scream. Then she picked the squirming rodent up by the tail, lowered it into her mouth and . . . well, you get the picture. *Ick!*

I glanced back at Sybil. The color was slowly draining back into her face. She looked at me. "Grr," she growled gratefully.

"Grrwelcome," I replied.

Chapter
Thirteen

From there the day proceeded uneventfully until I got to gym class. I'd been looking forward to gym, figuring Sybil and I could use the free period to work on themes for the homecoming celebration. I entered and climbed into the bleachers as I always did.

"Margot Jean Johnson, where do you think you're going?" It was the unmistakable throaty rasp of Mrs. Mars.

I wheeled around, surprised to find a very much alive Mrs. Mars standing in front of the class, a class consisting of zombies dressed in ugly green gym uniforms. The zombies leered up at me with hungry eyes.

"Be careful, Mrs. Mars. They're dangerous," I warned softly.

"Who's dangerous?" she bellowed.

"Why . . . them." I pointed in the direction of the zombies.

She shot the ghouls an incredulous stare. "What's Miss Johnson talking about?" she rasped.

Surprisingly, all the zombies took a step backward, as if they were afraid of her. Then it dawned on me. Sense memory, of course. These girls had been afraid of Mrs. Mars since before they'd come to Salesian. Her evil reputation was legend in every junior high and middle school in the area. As humans they'd never dream of challenging her. Now that they were zombies, something in their bones told them she was way more dangerous than they were.

"Remember our little pact? Note or not, you're mine." She wheezed.

"I think you need to check with Principal Taft." My voice rose with indignation. "I'm sure he'll tell you I am exempt from gym for the rest of the semester."

Cackling laughter burst from her lips. "Principal Taft?" The zombies all took another step back. "Principal Taft has no jurisdiction over *my* PE class."

"But . . . but . . . he's the principal."

"We're hitting the track in preparation for the state endurance exam this morning. I expect you'll be joining us, won't you, Miss Johnson?"

I wanted to scream, *Who cares about the state endurance exam? The school is overrun with zombies who eat live mice, and Principal Taft promised me I'd never have to participate in gym class ever again.*

Mrs. Mars was staring at me, her beady eyes boring into me. "Time's a wastin', Miss Johnson."

I looked at the zombies. While they were afraid of Mrs. Mars, they were beginning to eye me like a meaty meat burger. So without another word, I zombie walked to the locker room and changed into my uniform.

The state endurance exam consisted of four disciplines: abdominal strength, upper-body strength, endurance and flexibility, and aerobic capacity. For abdominal strength we did sit-ups, for flexibility we stretched, and for both endurance and aerobic capacity we ran around the track. However, to build upper-body strength, Mrs. Mars subjected her classes to the most archaic exercise known to man—climbing the ropes.

The ropes was an exercise probably invented in the sixteenth century by pirates, for their children to swing on to practice attacking ships. Unfortunately, Salesian is an old school, built way back in the days when teachers still thought of pirating as a viable occupation. Over time, most gym teachers had abandoned the exercise, but not Mrs. Mars. She must have gotten some sadistic pleasure from watching young, modern girls hoist themselves up to the ceiling on thick braided rope.

As much as I hated all exercise, I found the ropes downright insulting. Talk about a useless discipline. When does a high-powered business executive ever need to climb ropes? *Well, Miss Hufferwinkle, your corporate responsibilities will consist of overseeing the World Trade Bank, managing the Trump portfolio, and, oh yes, the ropes. You do know how to climb the ropes, don't you?* Ridiculous.

Gym class that day was a grueling forty minutes of hell. Mrs. Mars ushered us out to the track, where we stretched and then zombie ran in a tight pack around the quarter-mile oval, with her yelling, "Pick it up!" and "Get the lead out!" for the entire period.

On the bright side, I was able to observe a very important fact about zombies. They can't run no matter how hard they try. Even with Mrs. Mars spurring us on, the zombies moved stiffly around the track, their legs locked at the knees, their arms outstretched as if they were doing a bad imitation of Frankenstein. I thought back to my earlier crisis with the zombies in the corridor that morning.

Note to self: If you're ever in a tight spot with a zombie again—run.

That night Sybil and I sat on the edge of my bed going over the events of the day, everything from the mouse incident to the grueling gym class—and let's not forget about lunch.

"You know, I do believe I'm the best lunchroom monitor ever."

Now that Sybil had some power I couldn't shut her up. She had become the lunchroom Nazi.

"The cafeteria is usually so noisy you can't hear yourself think, but not with me on patrol. No siree. Have you ever heard the cafeteria so quiet?" She looked at me expectantly.

"No," I replied. *Do I point out that everyone in the cafeteria is a zombie, and that zombies don't talk?* And *that zombies by nature are predictably passive unless something disrupts their pattern?* "You were great," I added.

"Thank you very much," she said. A self-satisfied smile spread across her face. I should have left it at that and moved on to more important things. But my mouth had other plans.

"I didn't know being lunchroom monitor was such a big deal for you. When you first mentioned it I thought you were joking."

The smile vanished. "Excuse me? Joking?" she said through tight lips.

"I mean . . . lunchroom monitor. It's . . . kind of . . . dorky."

Her eyebrows pinched together; her lips turned down. "Why? Because *you're* not lunchroom monitor?"

I knew if I kept going things would only get worse. *Agree with her, agree with her, agree with her, agree with her.* But instead I said, "Why would I want to be lunchroom monitor? Puh-leeze!"

"Margot Jean Johnson, you just can't be happy for me, can you? I am always happy for you when you get things you want."

It was true. Sybil was always there rooting for me, cheering me on. And I *was* getting everything I'd ever wanted—Yearbook Committee, Homecoming Committee, head cheerleader, prom queen. It should have been enough. It should have been easy for me to be happy for her. She was a lunchroom monitor. We weren't competing. But the darkness that had risen inside me could only be happy for me.

"That's because the things I want make sense," I heard myself say.

She winced.

"I mean . . . come on, Syb. Lunchroom monitor?"

"I'm not just lunchroom monitor. I'm *head* lunchroom monitor. There's a difference!" she exclaimed. "I have a larger vision here. You just can't see it yet."

I couldn't believe it. I was in my second fight with my best friend. I took several deep breaths.

"Um, uhh . . . Sorry," I said. "Head lunchroom monitor—that's a big deal. I can't wait to see your *vision*." There! My mouth was finally back under my control.

"You ought to be sorry," she snapped. She sat at the edge of the bed sulking. The damage had been done. It was too late for a mere apology.

And now for a brief note about compliments: Everyone appreciates a good compliment: *"Your hair looks lovely today." "My, how that new dress flatters your figure."* But we girls take compliments to a whole new level. We live for them. And it doesn't matter if the person paying the compliment is lying and we know they're lying. All that matters is the compliment itself. We can't help ourselves. Compliments are our drug of choice.

I faced Sybil and said, "You're right. I am jealous. But can you blame me? You've whipped that cafeteria into amazing shape."

Compliment.

"I did?"

"Oh, yeah. And the look on your face when you're patrolling between the tables . . . Wow."

"Wow?" she repeated, trying to read my face, wondering if I was going to get her on the hook and then burst into laughter.

"Double wow. And where did you get that little badge?"

"I made it out of foil from gum wrappers." The corners of her mouth turned up into a small smile.

"You *made* that? Wow again."

Compliment!

"You like it?"

I nodded. "You're like the sheriff of the cafeteria." *Well, I wasn't going to sit there and call her the lunchroom Nazi—duh!*

Her smile broadened. "I *was* kinda cool today, wasn't I?"

"Cool? You had those zombies eating out of your hand. . . . Well, not eating out of your hand because if they were eating out of your hand they'd probably eat your hand, but you know what I mean. I could never do that. Sorry," I said with even more sincerity.

"It's okay, Margot. I understand." She patted my hand. "If you had become head lunchroom monitor I'd be jealous, too."

I stifled a snort. Hurtful words were bubbling up inside me, another attack of verbal diarrhea rising in my throat. I jumped up. "Be right back," I managed to say.

"Where are you going?"

I didn't answer. I couldn't. My teeth were pressed firmly against my tongue. I pointed, grunted, and zombie walked to the bathroom. As I moved away I realized I needed to keep the dark thing inside me under control. No telling what kind of trouble I'd find myself in if I didn't.

Chapter
Fourteen

 With the end of the semester coming in six short weeks Sybil and I decided to forgo the homecoming event and instead hold a Winter Dance at the end of the semester.

It would be a prom-like affair where we'd get dressed up and party the night away. And the girl who was crowned winter queen would be more than any ordinary prom queen. Her name would be etched in the annals of Salesian High School history forever, since there'd probably never be another one. And the best part—there were only two candidates. With Sybil still feeling guilty over the Dirk thing, I knew I was a shoo-in for the title.

Take that, Amanda Culpepper.

For the first time since seventh grade school was fun and exciting. I couldn't wait to get there each morning, and actually was sad when we went home at the end of the day. Classes were a breeze. The few teachers who remained were zombies. They growled and moaned and scrawled illegibly on the board while we students sat quietly until the bell rang. After a few days, however, this got boring, so Sybil and I began staying after school, poring over our teachers' lesson plans with a thirst for knowledge that surprised us. We even gave ourselves homework. We didn't mind. As the new it-girls we deemed our education important. Never before had we studied so hard. Never before had our education seemed so precious. With learning no longer being rammed down our throats, Sybil and I took it upon ourselves to ram it down our own throats.

One of our biggest kicks came from teasing the zombies. They were so gullible. One time we put a walkie-talkie in a student locker. Then we stood in a corner shouting taunts into another walkie: "Hey, you stupid zombie. Come on over here and bite me. I dare you." The zombies growled and groaned and angrily tore at the locker as we continued to taunt them. When they finally ripped it open we switched channels to another walkie in a different locker: "Hey, zombie, I'm over here now!" Priceless.

We gossiped about other students: "Did you happen to notice Amanda Culpepper's mole lately? I do believe it's growing an Afro."

"Did you get a whiff of her new cologne? Eau de Funky Armpits."

In the past, we wouldn't dare gossip about Amanda for fear it might get back to her. But now that she was a zombie, she was the target of daily ridicule. It felt so good to have the shoe on the other foot.

Sybil and I took turns giving the morning announcement each day from Principal Taft's office. Here's an example of one of mine:

"Cheerleading practice will begin promptly at two forty-five in the gymnasium. No zombies allowed. The new cheerleader uniforms, designed by me, Margot Johnson, will be unveiled in two weeks. The best thing about these uniforms is that they are not made for rail-thin, anorexic-looking girls like you see in the fashion magazines. These amazing uniforms are designed for real girls, who know they look good without starving themselves to death. The cheerleading squad looks forward to seeing you all at the unveiling. . . . And remember, no zombies will be allowed."

The "no zombie" rule was aimed squarely at Amanda.

Here's one of Sybil's:

"As you all know, lunch is the most important meal of the day. For this reason it is imperative that everyone move through the cafeteria in an orderly manner. Students will be seated by me. Any student, zombies included, not obeying the rules set forth by the head lunchroom monitor will be expelled from school for the rest of the semester. Thank you and have a nutritious day."

Despite the lack of student participation, high school was shaping up to be everything I'd hoped for.

My confidence was soaring. I was suddenly walking with my head held high. And with no one around to judge me I started wearing things I had once thought too risky to try under Amanda's watchful gaze: a black mini, a lime-green hoodie, brown suede boots with a spiked heel.

I thought back to the dark days when I constantly obsessed over my thighs, my arms, my stomach. What a waste of energy to go through life constantly looking over your shoulder, wondering if Amanda approved of how you looked that day, or if she was laughing at you. But the tables had turned, and I no longer cared what Amanda thought. She was a zero, a cipher in the universe of opinions that mattered.

I was now Salesian's it-girl, the queen bee. *Take that, Amanda Culpepper.*

A few days before Thanksgiving, Sybil and I were traveling in a pack of wannabe zombies when I noticed a pack of jock zombies heading toward us from the opposite direction. Amid the pack was Dirk Conrad.

"Ooh, there's Dirk," said Sybil.

We stared at him as the jock zombies slogged by. It was a sad sight. The left sleeve of his varsity jacket had been ripped off, obviously in some zombie skirmish, and the large embossed Knight's helmet that had proudly graced the right side of his chest hung on by a thread. His complexion was a hideous shade of green, and those once glacier-blue eyes were now crimson in color.

"Can you believe we actually wanted to go out with him?" Sybil shook her head sadly.

"Yeah," I said. "Heh-heh. Imagine that."

I'd been so caught up in my studies and committee work I hadn't thought about Dirk in weeks. But now that he was right here, less than twenty-five feet away, my feelings for him came rushing back. I stopped and eyed him as he continued down the hall. Then I did the strangest thing. I stepped from the pack.

"What are you doing?" Sybil whispered nervously.

A few slacker zombies hanging by the trophy case emerged from their catatonic stupor and zoned in on me.

"I have to do this, Sybil," I said. "I'll see you later."

"Do what?"

My response was a glance in the direction of Dirk and the retreating zombies.

"No," she said. "Come back."

But I couldn't. I waved good-bye and watched as Sybil and

her pack continued down the hall. "Follow the pack," she called. "Margot, for heaven's sake follow the rules!"

I looked on silently as they moved away. In a few moments they were out of sight, leaving me standing alone. Exposed.

The zombies from the trophy case began staggering in my direction. But the danger they presented didn't matter. My high school manifesto flashed through my mind: *I will have a boyfriend.*

I stared up the corridor in the direction of the jock zombies moving away. I zeroed in on Dirk. The ripped varsity jacket now seemed a cool, hip fashion statement. His complexion wasn't hideous at all, but a deep, swarthy, sexy green. And his eyes weren't crimson, they were a gorgeous shade of ruby red.

I will have a boyfriend.

I took off after Dirk at a dead run, leaving the slow-moving zombies from the trophy case flailing at me as I zipped by. My plan? I didn't have one. My newfound status at school had gone to my head. I felt invincible. I was running toward a pack of zombies, headed into danger, and I didn't care. I had almost everything I'd ever wanted, and now my final desire was in my sight.

I will have a boyfriend.

I sped up the corridor toward Dirk and the zombies infused with the determination to have it all: popularity, parties, winter queen, and yes . . . a boyfriend.

Chapter
Fifteen

 A few years ago, when I was thirteen and my brother Theo eight, my father got the bright idea that the four of us should go on an exciting, fun-filled family vacation. Jamaica, you ask? Paris? Hawaii? Disney World? Don't be silly. While those are places any normal parent might find exciting, my father chose a week-long cattle drive vacation in Wyoming.

"Wow!" Theo exclaimed as Dad popped the sales video into the VCR. Yes, you heard me, V-C-R. Don't ask. "Look!" Theo shrieked when horses and cows appeared on the screen. "That one has poop hanging out of its butt. That is so cool."

"Well, it's so something," I said, looking on in horror. "If I'm not a laughingstock at school yet, I'm sure this is just the thing I need to push me over the top."

For thirty long minutes, we watched families ride horses, herd cattle, eat grotesque-looking meals out of tin plates, and sleep in beds with blankets that appeared to be made of burlap. When the torturous video was finally over I asked my parents to do me a giant favor and murder me in my sleep. I was as good as dead if we went on that trip. Mercifully, my request put an end to the idea of any family vacation in the Johnson household.

Now, however, as I ran toward the jock zombies, something from that video played back in my mind:

When herding cattle you sometimes need to cut a calf off from the herd.

Suddenly I was grateful I hadn't walked out on the video or yanked it from the VCR and set it on fire. There was actually something instructional in that dumb sales video, and I was about to put it to use.

The bell for fourth period had just rung, and sense memory sent most of the zombies in the corridor lumbering off to class. Only the trophy case zombies following me and the jocks in front of me remained.

"Hey, zombies!" I called as I neared the jocks. The jock zombies slowly turned, their hungry eyes falling on me. *Great*, I thought. *I've got their attention.* Ignoring the fact that I was surrounded, I stood my ground as the zombies in front of and behind slowly closed in.

"That's it, fellas. Come to Mama."

When the two groups were practically in striking distance I ducked into the girls' bathroom to my right, making sure I didn't move too quickly. Cutting—as I'd learned in the cattle drive video—was a delicate maneuver.

The first part of the maneuver was to herd the cattle/zombies into a pen. I chose the large handicap stall in the girls' bathroom as my pen. I headed for the stall, making certain I didn't move too quickly. I needed to be just a few steps ahead of the slow-moving zombies. Once inside the stall, however, I moved at breakneck speed, hopping onto the commode, boosting myself up and quickly over the side, making sure I was out before the zombies started in.

The sluggish zombies began entering the stall.

I zombie walked back around to the entrance of the stall, joining the pack, pretending to be one of them pushing to get at me. But in truth, I was shoving zombies into the stall, making certain Dirk wasn't one of the zombies going in. Then, after all the zombies but Dirk were in, I slammed shut the stall door, jamming it with a wad of chewing gum. The zombies inside were too busy pushing forward to realize their escape route was behind them.

I turned to Dirk, who had successfully been cut from the pack. A soft moan emanated from deep in his chest.

"Mmmmmmmph."

His ghastly green fingers reached for me. His ruby red eyes gazed hungrily upon me as gobs of drool slithered down his chin.

Ohmygod! He's sooo cute!

"Come on, Dirk. We've got some training to do."

I pulled a hunk of raw ground beef from my Baggie and held it out to him. He lurched forward, grasping for the meat. I took a few quick steps backward.

"That's it. Follow me," I said as I lured him to the office of my guidance counselor, Miss Everheart.

Training a zombie is a lot like training a dog. You have to realize he only has one thing on his mind: food. To have success with zombies, the zombie must think of you as the sole provider of food when he does good, and punishment when he is bad.

Once in the office, I sat Dirk across from me and pulled out my supply of raw meat hunks and a rolled-up newspaper.

"Hello, boyfriend," I cooed.

Dirk growled, snatched up my hand, and tried sticking it in

his mouth. *Smack!* I swatted him across the nose with the rolled-up newspaper.

"Yeeeeee!" He let loose a high-pitched whine and shrank back. He gazed at me, fear dancing in his eyes.

"Okay," I said, brandishing the newspaper. "Let's try it again. Hello, boyfriend."

I dangled the hunk of meat in front of him. Cautiously, he took it from my hand, then gobbled it down. *Success,* I thought. It was Dirk's first step in becoming my boyfriend.

After that day life was even more perfect than before. Aside from the occasional boyfriend trying to kill me, I was living the dream. Most popular girl at school, chairperson of all the important committees, and to top it all off, I had a boyfriend.

*Top Ten Advantages
to Having a Zombie Boyfriend*

10. You will never catch him staring at a cute girl at the mall. (If he's staring at anyone it means just one thing—it's time for lunch.)

9. There's no competition for the remote. (You can eliminate the word ESPN from your vocabulary forever.)

8. He will never post embarrassing pictures of you on the Internet.

7. He will listen to you talk for hours on end without interrupting or falling asleep.

6. He will never cheat.

5. He will never forget your birthday. (He won't remember it either, but at least you won't be wondering, "Did he forget again?")

4. He will never stand you up on a date. (If you have meat, he will be there.)

E. Van Lowe

3. He will never try to convince you to go all the way. ("All the way" has a whole different meaning in zombieland. If you've gone all the way with him, welcome to the living dead.)

2. He will never choose his friends over you. (Zombies don't have any friends. If you provide him with meat, you're his lifelong pal.)

1. And the number one advantage to having a zombie boyfriend: You will never hear the words "We need to talk." (That's right, he will never, ever dump you. Yay!)

Chapter

Sixteen

 "Tryouts for holiday carolers are being held in the gym this coming Thursday afternoon. All interested students should come and bring your best singing voices. Hot apple cider will be served. No zombies allowed."

I finished the morning announcement and turned to Principal Taft. He was frowning at me.

"Did I say something wrong? I know it's a little early for caroling, but I thought I'd get a jump on things."

"No, no, you were perfect. It's just that—"

A storm of doubt raged in the pit of my stomach. "You don't want us caroling at all?" I said, interrupting.

"No, caroling is commendable."

"You don't like the cheerleader uniforms?"

"Glamorously gorgeous."

"My hair, my attitude, the way I run the committees?"

"Excellent, excellent, excellent."

"Then what am I doing wrong?"

"It's not you. You are doing everything right. But my supervisor, Mr. Pennyfield, loves our Holiday Pageant. I'm sure he'll want to stop by. And I was hoping you could cook up some little extravaganza for him."

"It will be a *little* extravaganza with only me and Sybil in it."

"See, that's a problem. He's going to ask why there aren't other students participating."

"Because they're zombies!"

"Right. But of course we don't want him to know that, do we? Margot, you're a terrifically talented young lady . . ."

Compliment!

"I know you can come up with something to convince him nothing is amiss at Salesian High. Am I right in trusting you with this responsibility?" He smiled into my eyes.

"Of course you are, sir."

"We're going to stage a huge holiday musical with *zombies*? Have you lost your mind?"

Sybil, Dirk, and I were seated in the cafeteria on our lunch break. We had become our own pack. No longer were we required to tag along with other zombie packs to get around school. With Dirk in our lives we had our own inner circle. Just the three of us.

Sybil was staring at me as if I'd gone bananas.

"We can do it. We'll hold the Holiday Pageant and a week later the Winter Dance. And the best part is Amanda Culpepper can't participate in either of them. She's gonna be so jealous."

"I hate to rain on your parade, Margot, but jealousy is an emotion—and zombies don't have any."

Amanda and the Twigettes were seated across the room at a table with some nerd zombies.

"Wanna bet?" I whispered. "Look at her." We glanced over

at Amanda. "She's glaring at us. She knows this is the first year she won't have the lead in the Holiday Pageant."

"No, I think she's eyeing that hunk of raw meat you just shoved into Dirk's mouth."

"I bet she wishes she'd bit us now." I scowled in Amanda's direction. "Well, it's too late," I mouthed. "Tough noogies. You had your chance. This school belongs to me now." I grinned at her like an eight-year-old with a brand-new Barbie, then slid my arm lovingly around Dirk's shoulder.

He tried to bite it. *Smack!*

"Yeeeeee!"

I turned to Dirk all apologetic. "Baby's sorry she had to do that to Snookie, but Snookie can't bite Baby." I pulled another hunk of raw meat from a Baggie and threw it to him. He grabbed the meat in midair and gobbled it up. "I taught him that," I said proudly.

"Snookie?" Sybil's lips twisted into a frown.

"That's what I call him—Snookie. I think it's cute when couples have pet names for each other."

"What does he call you—Lunch?"

"Sounds like somebody needs to sit over there with the other jealous girls."

"I'm not jealous of a zombie," Sybil barked. She folded her arms across her chest and began to pout.

"Good. Then you won't mind if I cancel tonight."

"What? Again? You canceled on me last night."

"Well, somebody's gotta choreograph the Holiday Pageant." I leaned in and lowered my voice. "Besides, I'm teaching Dirk something new, and he's a little slow."

"Oh? And what are you teaching him?" she asked through clenched teeth.

I fixed her with a firm, steady gaze. "Well, if you must know, I'm teaching him how to sing."

She stared back, her eyes narrowing. I could practically see slow wisps of steam rising off her forehead. "You're teaching a zombie to sing?" Her voice was low and filled with scorn.

"Yes. Christmas carols. As president of the Caroling Committee it's my job to make sure we have the best carolers the school has to offer. And in case you haven't noticed, we need a bass to offset your soprano and my alto."

"We cannot take Dirk caroling with us," she said, eyeing him with contempt.

"Why not?"

"Because instead of caroling Dirk will be consuming everyone in his path. He's a zombie, remember?"

I lowered my voice and again leaned in. "Don't be a name caller." I wagged a chastising finger at her. Then I turned to Dirk. "Hey, Snookie, wanna go for a walk before class?"

A low moan rose from deep in his chest.

"Me, too." I got up and faced Sybil. "We're the in-kids now, but remember where you came from, Syb. You didn't like anyone calling you names. Let's not become *them*," I said, throwing a glance over at Amanda and her green-with-envy ghoulfriends.

Sybil shook her head slowly. "You don't get it, do you?" she said, her eyes softening. "Margot, we have an opportunity to do something good this semester. We should be trying to make our time among the zombies mean something."

"I am doing something good. I'm teaching Dirk how to sing."

Sybil opened her mouth to say something more, but must have thought better of it because she closed her mouth and just stared.

A moment later Dirk and I blended into a pack of zombies

passing through the cafeteria. I didn't look back, but I was certain Sybil's eyes were burning a hole in the back of my head.

Later that evening, Dirk and I sat in my room. I was alternately feeding him scraps of ground beef and flipping through my songbook in search of just the right holiday songs for caroling. I felt a pang of guilt knowing Sybil was at home alone. But isn't that what an it-girl does—dump her friends for her boyfriend?

"Margot!" my brother Theo called from the other side of my bedroom door. "Are you guys eating in there? You know Mom doesn't allow food in the bedroom."

"We're not eating. And if we were eating it wouldn't be any of your business."

"I smell food," the little brat chimed.

"You smell your upper lip," I countered. Oh, how I wanted to yank open the door, tie a leg of lamb around his scrawny little neck, and let Dirk have at him. But the thought of Theo roaming the Earth forever sent a chill up my spine. I couldn't do that to the human race. "Go away," I called. "We're busy."

"Margot and Snookie sitting in a tree, k-i-s-s-i-n-g," he sang as he clomped off down the hall, snickering all the way.

A sudden emptiness drifted over me. If only Dirk and I could share a kiss. I sighed. Most girls spend half their lives romanticizing about their first boyfriend, wondering what the first kiss will be like. First kisses are important. Now that I had a boyfriend I had to face the reality that a kiss between us could never be. It's all right, I told myself. A girl can't have everything.

Technically I had my first kiss back in the eighth grade. Sybil thinks I did—with Percy Paulson. If she only knew it never came off.

Percy was this cute boy with sandy-colored hair and freckles. I met him at the walkathon for breast cancer that Sybil dragged me to soon after we'd met. Percy hung out with us the entire day, cracking jokes and keeping things lively. It was obvious I was attracted to him.

At the end of the day Sybil left us alone to exchange phone numbers. That was all we did, although I let her think something more happened.

Sixteen years old and I've never been kissed, I thought. That's a secret worth keeping.

"Grrwl," Dirk called, dragging my thoughts back to the present. I was out of meat scraps and he was eyeing my arm, drool running down his chin. I sighed again over the fact that kissing between us was a definite no-no.

"Wait here," I said, brandishing the newspaper. Then I left the room, making sure I shut the door, and raced down to the fridge, where I replenished my supply of raw ground beef. I couldn't have been gone more than five minutes, but when I got back to my room the door hung open. Dirk was nowhere in sight.

Frantically, I yanked open my closet door. "Dirk?" I dove under my bed. "Dirk?"

I stepped back into the corridor. *Theo*, I thought. *I'll kill him . . . if Dirk hasn't done it already.*

"Mmmmm." A throaty moan . . . coming from the living room. Bad. Very bad. Mom and Dad were in the living room.

"Grrwwwwl!"

Oh, no! That growl sounded feisty. I took off for the living room at a dead run.

Chapter
Seventeen

I love my parents. Despite all the horrible—albeit true—things I say about them, I love them dearly. Some of my fondest memories include them: my first Barbie doll, my first CD player, cash under my pillow when I lost a tooth, my first CD, my first trip to Six Flags, cash for every other trip to Six Flags, cash for more CDs, my first miniskirt, my first pair of heels, my first car. And while I had not yet received said car, I was expecting them to come through with one by the time I graduated. A royal blue Mustang convertible. Their demise would greatly hinder the prospect of that ever happening. So the pain of walking into our living room and finding them dead, or undead, would be almost too much to bear.

I peered into the living room. There they were: Dad, Mom, and Dirk, staring dazedly at a documentary on the Discovery Channel. A gob of bloody flesh hung from Dirk's lips.

"How could you!" I said loudly. Slowly, three heads swiveled in my direction. Three sets of eyes stared at me with distant, far-away looks.

"Mmmmmph," said Dirk.

And then to my surprise, my mother spoke. "Is something wrong, dear?"

Huh? It didn't make sense. Zombies can't talk. Can they? It was then that I saw Dirk's hand snaking into a bucket of fried chicken that rested on the couch between him and my father. He pulled out a thigh and bit into it with gusto. "Mmmmmph," he said again.

I shook my head. "Umm, no," is all I could muster.

All attention went back to the TV. It wasn't bloody flesh I'd seen hanging from Dirk's lips, but greasy fried chicken. A careful look into my parents' eyes revealed they weren't undead at all. The catatonic state I'd found them in was their typical catatonic state. This was how they spent most evenings, sitting zombie-like in front of the boob tube. Dirk had wandered in because he smelled the chicken, and he didn't bite them because . . . he assumed they were already zombies.

"Hmm," my father grunted at something that happened on the TV.

"Hmm," Dirk replied. He reached for another piece of chicken.

I was engulfed by a wave of hope as I observed Dirk seated on the sofa between my parents. He wasn't attacking them. They had no idea he wasn't anything but a normal, hungry teenager. Perhaps there was a chance for romance after all. Maybe Dirk would have the all-important first dance with me at the Winter Dance. And maybe, just maybe, he would be able to find the restraint to take me into his arms and kiss me without killing me.

I sighed. It was a tall order.

There were four weeks left in the semester, and I still didn't have an idea for the Holiday Pageant.

I have always loved the holidays. It is my favorite time of year. Roving bands of carolers roaming the streets of our town during the winter evenings, bringing cheer to all. When I was old enough to realize the carolers were all students from Salesian High, I told myself that when I attended Salesian I would become a caroler, too.

You can't imagine my joy when the announcement for carolers came during my freshman year. Twelve of us showed up that first day. A good-sized group. I envisioned us bundled up in our winter gear, singing together, laughing together, exchanging holiday gifts. Then Amanda Culpepper swept in, clutching the sign-up sheet. Upon seeing the group, she frowned.

"Oh, my. There's more of you than I expected." Her eyes pored over us, stopping occasionally as she pinched up her nose and twitched her head as if we all smelled.

"There were sixteen of us last year," a boy said.

"Hmm, really," Amanda responded, turning her gaze on the boy, eyeing him as if he were a new species she was observing for the first time.

"Yeah, but it all worked out. We just didn't sing so loud."

"Ohhh," Amanda said, a sardonic smile on her lips. "You thought that was a question. It wasn't. It was a statement, and what it meant was, last year was last year and this year is this year." She smiled at the boy—at least her lips arched into what should have been a smile, but it was a joyless expression.

"You can't turn people away. Everyone who shows up gets to carol. It's kind of a holiday tradition at Salesian. No one has to feel left out."

Amanda stared at him for a long moment. "Oh, was *that* a question?" Her voice dripped sarcasm. "If it was, the answer is *of course I can turn people away.* I'm chairman of the Caroling Committee. And I'm starting with you."

"But—"

"You're not even in the Glee Club. And from the whiny sound of your voice, singing is not your thing."

"But—"

"That's all. Thank you for coming. And by the way, that wasn't a question, either. It doesn't require a response. All it requires is for you to leave."

Beaten and humiliated, the boy and seven others slinked from the room. I was among the seven who didn't want to be personally humiliated by Amanda, so I left before she could turn her wrath on me.

But this year was different. This year Amanda would be the one at home turning up her TV to drown out the holiday sounds. . . . Okay, I know Amanda is a zombie who has no idea she's not being included in the festivities. I wish she did.

"'Frosty the Snowman'? That's not a Christmas carol," Sybil said.

We were in the school's choral room, supposedly rehearsing Christmas carols, but every time I suggested the perfect song, Sybil rejected it.

"I know. But it's a happy, wintry song," I said, turning my attention back to my list.

"So is 'Jingle Bells.' And we're not singing that."

"Actually, I was thinking of 'Jingle Bells' as well."

Without responding, Sybil turned to Dirk, who sat in a corner busying himself with a pile of mystery meat left over from lunch in the cafeteria. "Dirk, do you know 'Frosty the Snowman'?" she asked.

Dirk looked up at her, briefly cocking his head to one side. "Mmmph," he moaned before sticking his face back into the pile of lunchmeat.

"He doesn't know it." She turned to me and shrugged. "Sorry."

"Very funny, Syb."

"I'm not trying to be funny. His bass needs the perfect song to offset my soprano and your alto, right? I think it should be one of the carols you've been spending all your evenings teaching him."

"This is about us not hanging out lately, isn't it?"

"Don't be silly. You have a boyfriend now. No one expects you to hang out with your best friend since the eighth grade. It's just that since you've been spending so much time teaching Dirk to sing, I think we should concentrate on the songs you've already taught him. So, which ones are they?"

"Okay, Sybil. You've made your point. I've been a first-class jerk putting my relationship with a zombie ahead of my best friend . . ." is what I should have said.

Instead I said, "You're so selfish it's embarrassing. Here I am trying to do something nice for the community, and all you can think of is yourself." I knew I was lying. I knew I had short-changed her. But my mouth was once again operating under its own power, and the words just flew from my lips.

"*I'm* selfish?" said Sybil.

"There, you admitted it!"

"You know good and well who the selfish one is here, Margot. You're just too stubborn to own up to it."

"Am not!" Childish, I know. But when you're caught in a lie your mind goes primal . . . at least mine does.

"Are too!" It appears Sybil's mind had gone primal as well.

"Am not!" I threw my song list and music sheets into the air and got in her face.

"Are too!" She didn't back down. We were nose-to-nose.

"Sybil Mulcahy, you take that back or you are off the caroling team."

"Ooh, an alto singing with a bass who screeches and groans.
This is going to be the best caroling year ever. I can't wait to
hear you guys caroling in front of *my* house."

"Forget you, Sybil."

"Too late. You're already forgotten."

Ouch! "Oh, yeah?"

"Yeah!"

Without another word, I stormed from the room and raced
down the corridor. *Why couldn't I just admit I was wrong?*
Why couldn't I tell her I was sorry I hadn't been spending any
time with her? With no other humans around I knew she had
to be lonely. I certainly was.

Fueled by adrenaline, I raced through the school at top
speed, not knowing where I was going, not caring, just need-
ing to burn off my anger. Finally out of breath I stopped and
doubled over in a coughing, wheezing jag, struggling to catch
my breath.

"Mmmmmm."

The sound of a zombie. No, not one zombie, many zombies. Slowly, I lifted my head. I was standing at an intersection
in the corridor—surrounded. I'd gotten so worked up I'd run
from the room without my vial of fish oil or my rolled-up newspaper. I was stranded without any of my weapons against a
zombie attack—totally exposed.

"Mmmmmm." Zombies came at me from all four directions. This was different from the time I'd taken on the zombies to cut Dirk from the herd. This time there was no escape
route.

I took a step back. "Harumph!" The zombies behind me
seemed to delight in the fact I was making it easy for them.

They reached for me. I wheeled around, striking my fake karate pose. It had no effect. They continued to close in.

"Mmmmmuhh!" The zombies to my right were reaching for me as well, their arms outstretched, their lips parted in anticipation of the feast of flesh.

"Sybil!" I found myself calling. "Sybil, I'm surrounded by zombies. Help!"

Nothing. No sound of footsteps rushing to my aid, just the slow *swish-swish* of zombie feet dragging closer and closer.

"I deserve this," I said out loud. "If I hadn't dissed Sybil we wouldn't have gotten into the argument, and I wouldn't be here now."

I had precious little time to feel sorry for myself. A nerd zombie dug her hand into my shoulder. Instinctively I jerked away, only to find myself in the arms of a prep zombie. His lips parted.

"I'm sorry, Sybil," I whispered as I prepared to join the living dead. Tears streaked my cheeks as a horde of zombie hands clutched at my arms, tugging me in all directions. I tried pulling away, but I was no match for their number, their strength. I was a rag doll, slowly being ripped to shreds.

Suddenly, two sturdy zombie hands gripped me by the shoulders from behind and began pulling me backward. Something, a bag, went over my head.

"What the . . . *HELP!*"

Darkness.

"I've got her," a zombie voice said. "Let's get out of here."

I could feel myself flying backward, *faster . . . faster . . . faster. . . .*

Chapter

Eighteen

 "Watch her head."

"I got it."

Thump. "Ow!"

"I told you to watch her head."

"You're not the boss of me."

This back-and-forth went on for a full five minutes as the two zombies—or whatever they were—transported me away. By the time they set me down on a chair and removed the hood, I recognized one of the voices.

"Hello, beautiful," Baron Chomsky crooned as the hood came off. It was a poor attempt at sounding cool, but I didn't care how geeky he sounded. Baron Chomsky had saved my life.

"Baron!" I cried, looking around, trying to make sense of what was happening. "You're not a zombie."

"Nope," he said, grinning at me.

"You're not a zombie, either, and we want to know why," came the voice of the other boy in the room—Milton Sharp. The cartoon character on the T-shirt he wore today was a cricket, standing upright like a human, with a bad case of the shakes.

"We know why," said Baron, turning to Milton. "Leave her alone."

We were in a dusty old storage room in the basement that had been converted into a science lab.

" 'Leave her alone' said the big-shot know-it-all. Well, homie, you may have just signed our death warrant. I hope you're happy," called Milton. He paced quickly back and forth, eyeing me suspiciously.

"What's going on?" I asked.

Milton stopped pacing. "Why aren't you a zombie?" His eyes tore into me. "I'll tell you why, because *you* are the zombie master. And now you know where our hideout is, and you're going to bring your friends here to kill us." He wagged an accusing finger in my direction.

"Milton, that's ridiculous."

"It's the reason we threw the hood over your head," Baron said. He seemed embarrassed for his friend. "Sorry about that, but he wasn't sure about you, so he didn't want you to know where our hideout is."

I looked around at the room. "Hideout?"

"Big mistake removing that hood, homie," Milton called.

"Ignore him. He's read one too many comic books."

"And it's a good thing I have, otherwise we wouldn't have found the cure." Milton started pacing again, eyeing me with contempt. "Didn't know we had an antidote, did ya?"

I shook my head, turned to Baron. "Can somebody please tell me what on Earth is going on here?"

"Why did she say 'Earth'?" Milton asked, his voice rising with suspicion. "Is the zombie master an alien?"

"Idiot!" cried Baron. "If she had control over them would we have had to rescue her?"

Milton stopped, his face twisting into a pout as he thought about this for a moment. "Don't call me an idiot. I have a four-point-oh GPA."

"And you never let me forget it."

"You guys aren't zombies, either," I said.

"Not yet!" said Milton. "But now that you're here . . . ," he added, rolling his eyes.

"We believe the transformation happened at the carnival. And since we didn't go that night we were spared being infected," said Baron. "We've been roaming the school ever since, hiding and studying the zombies while we searched for a cure. This storage room is our base of operation."

"I didn't go to the carnival, either," I said. "Sybil and I went to the carnival grounds the night after to look for clues, but the carnival was gone."

"See?" Baron said. "She's on our side."

"You were at the location where Patient Zero got infected?" Milton asked, eyeing me skeptically.

"Patient Zero?"

"That's who he calls the first person to get infected."

"Oh." Baron was smiling at me. I smiled back. It felt good talking to a real person other than Sybil or Principal Taft for a change.

"I don't believe her," Milton said suddenly. "I've been watching you. You sure act like you're in charge of them, parading around school like . . . like *the zombie master*. I think you're behind it."

A tiny bit of the anger from the choral room reared up. "Why do you keep saying I have something to do with the zombies?" I barked, advancing on him. He wasn't expecting my sudden aggression and shrank back.

"Because," he said, his voice turning whiny and defensive, "you're not one of them." He took a few more steps backward, making a cross of both his index fingers and thrusting them at me as if to hold me at bay.

"Neither are you!" I took a step toward him and his silly cross. "By the way, crosses are for vampires."

"Okay, stalemate," called Baron, jumping between us. "We believe somebody released a microbe into the air."

"Who would do such a thing?"

"Who indeed!" chimed Milton.

"Look, we're all here for the same reason, to find a way to make our classmates normal again. I'm glad you're not one of them," Baron said, his voice softening. I could feel myself beginning to blush—which didn't make any sense since the sweet sentiment was coming from a geek.

"So you have a cure?" I said, changing the subject.

"Yes!" exclaimed Milton.

"Not exactly," said Baron. "We're working on the antidote."

"Dude! Do not give military intelligence to the enemy," Milton whispered through his teeth.

I turned to Baron. "Your friend is a real pill."

"I know, and the worst kind of pill—a pill with a four-point-oh GPA."

I smiled at him. It was the first time I could ever remember me and Baron agreeing on anything. Go figure.

"Say what you want, but we're on a mission to turn our classmates normal again, and *you* had better stay out of our way." Milton was staring at me, trying to look ominous, and failing miserably at it.

"Knock yourselves out," I replied. "And as far as being in your way goes, *you* brought me here."

"*He* brought you," Milton said, pointing to Baron. "And now it's time for you to go."

A short time later, they returned me to the choral room, where I found Sybil and Dirk as I'd left them. I told Sybil about the zombie attack, the rescue, and the fact that Baron and Milton were still among the living.

"Really? Where are they now?" she asked.

"I'm not sure. They dropped me off outside the door and took off."

"Uh-huh. I wonder why they didn't stop in."

"One of them said something about remaining in hiding." The truth is, Baron had said, "We're stealth bombs for justice, baby." Then he had tried to kiss me on the cheek, but that corny line didn't deserve a kiss.

"And you have no idea where their hideout is?" I could tell from the tone of Sybil's voice she thought I was lying.

"No. They put a hood over my head." I explained Milton's paranoia.

"Right. The geeks who rescued you from the zombies put a hood over your head because they thought you were the zombie master. Makes sense to me."

"Sybil, it's the truth."

"Of course it is, Margot. I'm sure you're not saying it just to make me feel sorry for you so I'll let you have your way." She patted my hand. "I know you wouldn't do anything like that." She shot me a sarcastic smirk. "Now, while you were on your *adventure*, Dirk and I went over the carols he knew."

She handed me the sheet of loose-leaf paper she'd been

writing on: "O Come All Ye Faithful," "O Little Town of Bethlehem," "O Tannenbaum."

O-O-O. We were right back where we started.

"A marvelously merry Monday morning to you, young ladies."

Sybil and I were in Principal Taft's office. We had just finished the morning announcement.

"It is a merry morning," I said with a smile. I was now the school's fashionista, dressed in a hot pink, skintight, hoodie warm-up suit with green writing on the butt. And there was no one around to tell me I looked fat in it.

"I think this whole zombie thing is going rather well." Principal Taft beamed at us. "So, how's the Holiday Pageant coming along?"

"Um . . . excellent," I said. Sybil rolled her eyes.

"You do remember Pennyfield is coming?"

"Yes, sir. And he will never suspect that anyone in the pageant is a zombie."

"Good." Taft turned to Sybil. "And how are things going with you?"

"Very good, sir. The cafeteria is running like a well-oiled machine. With me on patrol, everyone is toeing the line." Her words hung in the air as she thumped her gum foil badge to punctuate the statement. I rolled *my* eyes.

"Excellent, excellent, excellent," Taft said with a big grin. He rubbed his hands together. "I knew you were the right girls for the job."

"And we have a wonderful group of carolers this year," Sybil suddenly said. "You should hear Snookie's bass. It's enough to make you cry."

My head snapped around. *"Snookie?"*

"I saw you rolling your eyes at me," she said with a pro-nounced glare.

"Well, excuse me, Marshal Mulcahy. What are you going to do, ban me from brunch?"

"You think you're so smart. And I thought we didn't like girls who wore skintight warm-up suits with writing on the butt?"

"For your information this is a holiday outfit, and holidays get an exemption."

"Of course they do, Amanda—I mean, Margot."

"What did you call me?"

"If the skintight warm-up suit fits . . ."

"Ladies! Is everything okay between you two?" Taft inter-rupted.

"Yes!" we both barked.

"Because it sounds like it isn't."

I looked at Sybil, wondering if she was going to tell him about our caroling issue, and that I had no idea what to do for the Holiday Pageant.

"No, we're cool," she said. I breathed a sigh of relief.

"Yeah," I said, "just a little fashion disagreement."

Principal Taft's eyes moved from me to Sybil and back as he tried to determine the depth of the rift between us. We stared back, blank defiance on our faces. We'd both been here with adults before, including parents and teachers. What happens between kids stays between kids.

And now a brief note to adults about trying to read our minds: This is a potentially dangerous activity. I once heard of a parent who figured out how to read her daughter's mind. When she finally got inside, the poor woman's head exploded—literally. Her brain couldn't handle the weight of all those mixed-up teenage thoughts. True story. So adults, please, stay out of our heads. It's for your own good.

Anyway, after a few moments staring into our blank faces, Principal Taft gave up. Finally he said, "I can't wait to see what you've done for the Holiday Pageant."

"That makes two of us," said Sybil with a sarcastic smile.

I wanted to smack her.

The fall semester was drawing to a close. Mrs. Mars stepped up her campaign to get us in shape for the state endurance exam. We ran, jumped, and did push-ups all period long. The woman was fixated on us all passing the silly exam.

One day when I got to the gym, the ropes had been made ready for us to climb. Four thick, braided ropes hung from the ceiling to the floor. I gaped at them in horror.

While the zombies had all made a feeble attempt at running around the track, not one of them had the ability to climb the rope. One by one they each stepped up to the rope, and failed miserably at any attempt to climb.

Finally it was my turn. I stepped up to the rope.

Mrs. Mars looked up from her clipboard. "Climb all the way to the top, touch the bar, and shimmy back down," she barked.

"Why do I have to climb? None of them did."

"I judge each student on her individual ability, Miss Johnson. Now, climb."

I looked up. The ceiling had to be forty, fifty feet off the floor. "I don't have the ability to climb, either," I snapped.

"Margot Jean Johnson, get on that rope, and get on that rope now!" Mrs. Mars said, her face turning red.

The zombies around me inched back.

I gripped the rope and began to climb. Pain seared through

my fingers and up my arms. My puny muscles were like kindling that had just been set on fire.

"Higher!" Mrs. Mars called.

I looked down. I was only a foot and a half off the floor when I realized I could go no farther.

"I can't!" I cried.

"Higher!" she insisted.

I tried pulling myself up, but my arms gave out. I dropped back to the floor.

Mrs. Mars eyed me with contempt. "Is that the best you can do, Miss Johnson? That's pathetic."

"I tried, Mrs. Mars, I really did."

"Same bat time, same bat channel," she rasped. Then she turned her attention back to her clipboard. "Next!"

The next time I had gym I didn't change into my uniform. Instead, I went right to the bleachers.

"Margot Jean Johnson, aren't you lonely up there in the bleachers all by yourself?" Mrs. Mars called.

"I *am* lonely up here," I called back. "But what can I do? Read my note."

Dear Mrs. Mars,
Please excuse our generous daughter, Margot, from
participating in gym class today. Yesterday after school
she was doing volunteer work at the hospital, where we
fear she may have picked up a touch of the Ebola virus.
We have been advised to keep her off strenuous activity so
that she doesn't bleed out and die. Your help in this will be
greatly appreciated.

Sincerely,
Mrs. Trudi Johnson

"You need to stop with these notes, Margot. You need all the work you can get," she said, and then she turned her attention to the class.

To my surprise, Sybil was really getting into the strenuous activity. She said it was because she didn't want an F in Phys Ed on her record.

That permanent record stuff some teachers try to pull on us is a hoot. Like there's really a record following us around from grade school throughout our lives—please! *Well Miss Wonderful, you've fed the world's homeless, ended all war, and cured cancer . . . Wait! What's this? You shot a spitball at Tommy Salami in the third grade. Tut-tut, I'm afraid we cannot give you the Nobel Peace Prize.* Yeah, right.

Yet Sybil claimed she was worried about failing gym. I didn't believe it. Sybil was reacting to the fact I had a boyfriend and was achieving my dreams. This was just another display of her jealousy. As much as I didn't want to admit it to myself, our friendship was slowly coming to an end.

 The next day, Sybil, Dirk, and I were cruising through the halls on our way to English.

"Did you see that?" Sybil asked. "That zombie just winked at you."

I swiveled my head slowly, so as not to call attention to myself. "That's not a zombie, Sybil. Look again. That's Baron Chomsky."

She stared at the zombies slowly moving through. Baron was shambling along midpack, a playful smirk on his lips.

"But . . . but . . . how is it possible?"

"I suppose I should know since I am *the zombie master*."

Her face turned several shades of red. "But . . . I'm so sor— I thought . . ."

"I know. Come on. I think he wants us to follow him." Baron was subtly giving us a hand signal behind his back.

Our little pack veered off course, following him down to the basement. Slowly the halls emptied as zombie students entered their classrooms along with zombie teachers. After a short while our two packs were the only ones in the corridor. I noticed Baron pointing at something.

"What is it?" whispered Sybil.

"Check out the zombie boy in front of him." The jock zombie in front of Baron had been given the world's biggest wedgie. The zombie's underwear had been hiked up practically to his chest.

For as far back as I could remember, geek boys had always been the target of bigger boys for a wedgie. Baron was getting even for every geek in America.

The jock zombie pack arrived at the weight room and entered while Baron hung back. As soon as they were all in, he pulled the door shut. Then, he turned to us as if he'd done something heroic, and struck one of his James Bond poses. "The name's Chomsky. Baron Chomsky."

Despite his silly antics I caught myself smiling.

"Dude! I told you not to bring them here!"

"But we need their help."

We were once again in Baron and Milton's basement hideout. Milton had hung a sign on the door that read THE FORTRESS OF SOLITUDE. Could he get any geekier? Upon entering we found Milton cooking up a chemical concoction over a Bunsen burner. Today's T-shirt featured a cow dressed as a gunslinger ready to draw on an opponent. COWBOY COW was written underneath the cartoon. When he noticed us, Milton stopped working, removed the beaker from the fire, and secreted it into a cabinet.

"We don't need anybody's help, homie," he said, eyeing me with distrust. "I told you, I got this."

"Well, alrighty then. See ya." I started from the room.

"Wait, wait," Baron called.

"Look, guys, I don't need to go through this again. If Milton doesn't want us here, we don't want to be here. Now if you don't mind, we're off to English class."

"Mmmaghhh!" Dirk emitted a hungry moan.

"We are totally breached, homie!" Milton cried with alarm. He threw his hands into the air. "He's signaling the troops. Pretty soon we're gonna be swimming in zombies."

I tossed a hunk of raw meat in Dirk's direction. He grabbed it mid-flight and gobbled it down. Satisfied for the moment, he stood patiently waiting for more.

I turned to Milton. "He's not signaling anyone. He's just hungry, that's all."

"See?" Baron said with a smile. "That's why we need her. She's the only one who can get close enough to them to get what we need."

"What is it you need?" Sybil asked.

"Ixnay on the DNA," Milton breathed through clenched teeth.

"DNA?" asked Sybil.

"Huh? That's not what I said."

"Yes," replied Baron. "We need some zombie DNA. Preferably saliva and a hair sample."

Milton threw up his hands. "We're dead."

"Could you help us out?" Baron's hazel eyes looked into mine.

How long have his eyes been hazel? I wondered. I looked away.

"You'd be doing us a big favor," he added.

"Okay. I can get you both hair *and* saliva. But what are you going to do for me?"

Baron smiled. "What do you want, baby?"

While I didn't want to participate in dezombifying my

classmates, recently I'd been cooking up an idea for the Holiday Pageant, and I was going to need lots of help to pull it off. "I need your help with the zombies for the Holiday Pageant."

"You got it," Baron said quickly.

Milton's eyes widened. "You can't put zombies in the Holiday Pageant."

"Sure I can. I'm president of the Holiday Pageant Committee, and I want zombies." Of course I didn't *want* zombies, but I wasn't going to tell him that.

He turned to Baron. "I told you she was the zombie master. Dude, you have been blinded by love."

"I know," said Baron. "Ain't love grand?"

Milton shrugged hopelessly. "We're dead."

"While we're helping you, Milton and I can keep our eyes peeled for the person who's responsible for turning everyone into zombies."

A look passed between Baron and Milton.

I pulled out a few hunks of meat and dangled them in front of Dirk.

"Mmmmph!" he moaned. His lips parted, and saliva drizzled down his chin, dripping to the floor.

"Is that enough?" I asked as I tossed Dirk the meat.

"More than enough," Baron said as Milton sucked up the spittle with an eyedropper.

Sybil looked on with disgust. "Gross!"

I turned to Baron. "Are you sure you guys know what you're doing?"

"Why do you ask, because we're just goofy high school students?" Milton snarled.

"Well . . ." I left the question hanging. I was certain the geeks could not create an antidote, which is why I was so willing to help. I'd get what I wanted, and they'd get . . . nothing. Perfect.

"Biology, chemistry, and a heavy dose of comic books," said Baron with a knowing smile. "You'd be surprised what a guy armed with that arsenal can do."

"And let's not forget we've got a four-point-oh GPA on our side." Milton again, as if being smart was the answer to everything. The only thing being smart guaranteed you in high school was a seat at the geeks' table. But if they wanted to think they could help our zombie classmates, who was I to stop them?

As Dirk was wolfing down the meat scraps I stepped behind him and yanked a clump of hair from his head. It came out easily. He didn't even flinch. When I handed the hair clump to Milton I noticed it was still attached to a tiny piece of scalp.

"Ewww!" Sybil said, as she made gagging sounds.

Milton gazed at the hair and saliva samples as if he'd just struck gold. "Now all we need are the samples from before he was a zombie."

"Excuse me?" I gazed at Baron, wide-eyed.

"Oh, right," said Baron. "I forgot to mention that to successfully create the antidote we'll need hair and saliva samples from Dirk while he was still among the living."

"Issue number two thirty-four of *The Cosmic Avengers*," Milton added.

"Where in the world are we supposed to find something like that?" I asked.

Baron was grinning at me. "You leave the rest to me. All you have to do from here on in is look beautiful. Like I said, the name's Chomsky . . . Baron Chomsky."

Geek city . . . although I have to admit that when he did the British accent this time, it was actually kind of cute.

That evening, after dinner, the four of us traipsed over to Dirk's house in the hopes of uncovering a hair and saliva sample from before he'd become a zombie. I had no idea what was in store. Would we discover Dirk's parents and sister were now among the living dead and waiting to ambush us? I tried not to think about it. If I wanted the geeks' help with the Holiday Pageant I needed them to believe I was on their side.

I'd never been to Dirk's home before, never met his parents, never been invited to his room. I tingled with anticipation. While the others had DNA samples on their minds, all I could think was that I was about to meet my boyfriend's parents for the first time. I had to make a good impression . . . which is why I brought flowers.

"What are those for?" asked Sybil.

"Dirk's mom."

"Suppose she's a zombie?"

"I have a two-piece value meal in my purse."

Sybil released a loud sigh. "When are you going to give up on the idea that a zombie could possibly be your boyfriend?"

"On our wedding day, I suppose."

She gave another loud sigh, this one filled with exasperation.

"You look really cute in that hooded parka," Baron said, sidling up next to me.

"Thanks." I caught myself smiling, but that was only because I appreciated the compliment.

Sybil looked from Baron to me and moved away.

"You nervous?" he asked.

"No." That wasn't entirely true. But I wasn't going to tell him I was nervous about meeting my boyfriend's parents.

"You're one heck of a girl, Margot." It sounded like a statement right out of the sixties, and yet coming from Baron it seemed just right. "I'm glad the zombies didn't get you." He was smiling at me again.

"Let's just get this over with," I said quickly. I needed to keep my mind clear for the operation.

It had begun to snow, a light dusting. It was the first snow of the year. The streets were empty, and our feet made a soft crunching sound as we walked. Baron walked by my side. I'd always felt that the first, quiet moments of a snowfall were incredibly romantic. I'd often envisioned myself walking along, holding hands with the special boy in my life and feeling like we were the only people on the face of the Earth. Too bad I was walking with Baron instead of Dirk—although I have to admit, it didn't seem the nightmare I once might have thought.

We arrived at Dirk's front door. Baron spoke. "Okay, now remember, if they're all zombies we represent a pack. If we stay together and do the zombie thing we're good." He smiled and gave me a wink. I made a prune face. "Then when they're not looking, one of us will slip away and go up to Dirk's room and search for his hairbrush and toothbrush."

Milton pulled a pair of walkie-talkies from his backpack. "This is how the one who slips away will stay in touch with the group." He handed me a walkie-talkie and was about to pocket the other.

"What are you doing? I'm the one who's gonna slip away," said Baron.

"We didn't agree on that," said Milton.

"We didn't have to agree. This is my caper."

"They're *my* walkie-talkies," countered Milton.

"I don't care whose walkie-talkies they are. I'm the one who's going to do the cloak-'n'-dagger stuff and that's final. Besides, you can't handle zombie combat. You're afraid of Margot."

Milton's face reddened. "I'm not afraid of a girl!" he squawked.

"You're afraid of your own shadow."

"I've got a four-point-oh GPA!"

"That doesn't stop you from being a sissy!"

"Is somebody out there?" came a female voice from the other side of the door. Before we knew it, the door was swinging open. I snagged the other walkie-talkie and handed it to Sybil. We hid them behind our backs just as the door opened on Dirk's mother.

"Hi," she said cheerily. She had dark hair like Dirk and a pleasant face. A puzzled look came over her as she stared out at us—two geek guys and two girls who didn't look like cheerleaders. "Are you kids friends of Dirk's?"

"Yes," snapped Milton, in an attempt to seize control of the moment.

"Oh?" she replied, looking Milton up and down. "What team are you on?"

"The chess team," he said, and shot us a look that implied he was brilliant.

We all shot him the stink eye.

"This is a joke, right?" Mrs. Conrad said, her voice laced with skepticism. "What do you kids want?" The door inched shut.

"You caught us, Mrs. Conrad," I said, giving a quick but hearty laugh. I eased in front of Milton. "Actually, we're Dirk's tutors. But we like to put you parents on from time to time. Gotcha!" I laughed some more. She stared at me cautiously for a moment, but eventually she smiled and pulled the door open wider.

"I didn't think Dirk knew how to play chess. You kids had me going there," she said with a chuckle. "So, four tutors. I didn't realize he was doing that badly."

"He's not. But since Dirk is a top athlete the school just wants to make sure he's getting all the help he needs." The words came tumbling out of me. I hoped they made sense.

"We need to tutor him right now," Milton said suddenly.

Her eyes were on him again. "What subject do you tutor?"

I held my breath and knew Baron and Sybil were doing the same.

"Calculus?" It was more a question than a statement.

Mrs. Conrad stared at him hard for a moment, and I knew she saw right through us and was about to slam the door in our faces. Then suddenly she burst into laughter. "You kids are such kidders. Come on in. Dirk hasn't had any visitors for such a long time. I'm glad to see he's getting help with his studies."

And we were in.

Chapter

Twenty

Mrs. Conrad led us toward the rear of the house. We passed the den, where we glimpsed Dirk's father sitting, watching TV. "Let's not disturb Mr. Conrad," she whispered as we passed. "Lately he's become very serious about his TV watching."

We glanced in the room as we eased by the door. Mr. Conrad sat as still as stone, staring vacantly at the TV. I shot a quick look in Sybil's direction. I know we were thinking the same thing. Mr. Conrad was a member of the living dead. We continued down the hall.

"Mmmmmph." A guttural groan from the den. We all froze.

"Coming, dear. I think he's ready for his dinner," Mrs. Conrad whispered. "Dirk is in the basement. He has a weight room down there. That's where he spends all his time lately. You kids go on down. I have to see to Mr. Conrad."

She pointed to the basement door, then scurried off to the kitchen.

Her husband and son were both zombies, and she had no idea. I felt sorry for her. Overnight her world had changed, and yet she ignored all the signs, clinging to how it once was, how she needed it to be. I'd heard about people like her, parents whose kids were killers and yet they blindly clung to the sweet image of their sons or daughters when they were innocent four-year-olds. Women whose husbands had lost all interest in the marriage and ignored them, yet the wives pretended that life was a bed of roses. Denial.

"Gimme the walkie-talkie." Milton's words brought me back. He was holding his hand out to me.

"No way!" I said. "I'm the one who's going up to Dirk's room." Can you blame me? I couldn't allow these strangers to pick over my boyfriend's things. Not before I had a chance to pick over them myself.

"You can't. You're a girl. It's too dangerous. There could be other zombies up there," Milton said.

"No problem. I'm the zombie master, right?"

Baron chuckled. "That's my girl."

Milton stared at me. Then he sighed. He could tell from the look on my face he wasn't going to win this one. "We need his hairbrush *and* his toothbrush," he said, clinging to authority.

"Got it."

"And if you get in any trouble call us."

"I will."

"So, I guess we're going down to the basement," Baron said. Milton eyed the basement door, fear dancing in his eyes.

"You go. Somebody's gotta be the lookout," he said, his eyes never leaving the door. "Lookout's a dangerous job, but I'll do it. I'll wait here, and if any zombies attack, I'll handle them while you guys are having your look around."

"That's a good idea," Baron said, allowing Milton to save face. He looked at me. "Be careful, beautiful. And give us a holler if anything goes wrong. Trouble is my middle name."

"Thanks," I said with a nervous smile. He squeezed my hand, and I felt myself blushing, which seemed strange. I attributed it to mixed-up emotions. Any girl would be a ball of raw nerves visiting her boyfriend's bedroom for the first time. I started upstairs.

When I reached the second-floor landing my ears were assailed by the sound of thumping pop music. I looked down the hall. There were three doors. One had a sign that read KEEP OUT! THIS MEANS YOU. The loud music was coming from behind this door. Dirk's sister's room, I thought. The next door had one of those DO NOT DISTURB doorknob hangers you see on the doorknobs of hotel and motel rooms. It was flipped around to the MAID SERVICE side. The parents' room no doubt. The doorknob hanger was to keep the kids from entering without knocking. Been there, done that. The third door had no markings, nothing to distinguish it from any other bedroom door in America. I knew it was Dirk's.

I don't know what I expected to find in Dirk's room, yet still I was surprised by what was there—nothing much, really. I guess I envisioned his dresser and shelves overflowing with trophies and medals. After all, he was one of the best athletes in the state. I pictured his walls covered with posters of all his sports heroes. Wrong. The room was surprisingly free of ego-stroking paraphernalia. There was only one tiny trophy on his dresser. It was from Little League. Next to the trophy was a photograph of ten-year-old Dirk in the classic batter's pose. He stared into the camera with little-boy charm. He was sooo cute. I was proud he was my boyfriend.

On his wall hung his science fair certificate along with two framed magazine photos of famous sports stars. One of John Elway and the other of Magic Johnson, but neither featured the sports stars in their uniforms. Instead both were wearing business suits. The framed articles that accompanied the photos were about the athletes after their careers were over and they had become successful businessmen.

A strange feeling washed over me. There was more to Dirk than just sports. Being here in his room allowed me to see into his soul. He played the role of jock in school for his friends and classmates. He played it well, but he'd actually given some thought to his life after his sports career was over. I felt vindicated for believing that Dirk wasn't a complete bubblehead. I envisioned us sitting on the edge of his bed and chatting about our futures. But that could never happen if he remained a zombie.

I moved to his dresser, found his hairbrush, and yanked out the hairs snagged between the bristles. I folded them into a slip of paper and put it in my purse. Now all I had to do was stop by the bathroom on my way downstairs and grab his toothbrush.

I was starting for the door when I noticed something on his bed. It was a button—one of those photo buttons you have made at carnivals. I moved to his bed, picked it up, and stared at the photo. Dirk and Amanda Culpepper stared back. It had obviously been taken at the carnival before everyone became zombies. My heart skipped. Dirk looked so happy. *How could anybody be happy dating Amanda?* I told myself it was too early in their relationship for him to know what a cow she was. Amanda's eyes burned defiance at me. It was as if she were saying, *See how happy he is with me? He'll never be that happy with you.*

Suddenly I felt I didn't belong there. It was like the air was being sucked from the room and I needed to get out or I'd never breathe again. I stuffed the button into my purse and hurried out.

As I stepped from the room into the corridor an icy zombie

hand sprang from nowhere and seized me by the throat. I tried to scream, but the vise-like grip pressed against my windpipe.

"Hhhhh." The grip tightened, stifling whatever sound I was trying to make. I wriggled and writhed in an attempt to break free, but it was no use. The zombie had the strength of ten men.

I'd gotten careless. I knew better than to step into an empty corridor when zombies were around. I'd given my meat scraps to Sybil, and the walkie-talkie in my purse was useless since I couldn't scream. The end was near. I gasped and sputtered as my air supply dwindled. A thick fog settled over my mind, blanketing my thoughts. One thought was clear, though. In a moment I'd be dead.

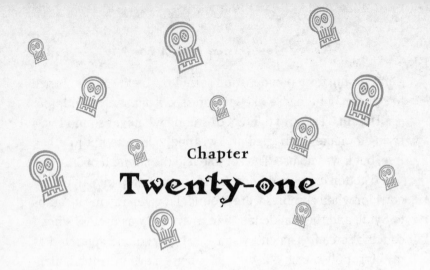

Chapter
Twenty-one

As the light of life drained out of me, Amanda's face drifted up through the fog. It was the face on the button, burning defiance. The face came to life and laughed at me. "Poor, pathetic Margot. I'll miss your designated dodging." At that moment putrid zombie breath wafted up my nostrils, and the very real face of Dirk's sister came into view. She had once been a teenybopper with freckles and a close-cropped haircut she'd probably seen on one of her idols in *Teen People* magazine. Now she was a zombie.

And she was about to bite me.

I marshaled what strength I had left and swung with all my might. In my excitement over visiting Dirk's home I'd forgotten to give the bouquet of flowers to his mother. Good thing. The flowers now hit Dirk's sister in the face just as her teeth were about to make contact. She bit down hard, but instead of flesh she got a mouthful of thorny stems. Her jagged teeth cut through the bouquet like butter. *Caarunchh!*

The mouthful of flowers surprised her, and she eased her grip on my windpipe. Air and lucidity rushed in.

I yanked away and raced down the hall.

"Weeeeeeeoooo," she cried as she staggered after me. I was at the landing when I remembered my mission: Dirk's toothbrush. I turned back and zipped up the corridor toward her. I dodged as she reached for me. After all, I was the designated dodger. I could dodge a soft rubber ball hurtling toward my head at fifty miles an hour. A slow-moving, teenybopper zombie was no match for me.

I ducked into the bathroom and slammed and latched the door behind me.

Kathump. The dead weight of Dirk's sister's body crashed into the door.

I moved to the counter. There were four toothbrushes on the rack. Finding Dirk's was going to be tough.

Kathump.

The ones that had been rinsed thoroughly after use belonged to the parents. That part was easy, but two gunky brushes remained.

Kathump.

One blue, one green. No giveaway there. I picked each up and examined it, slowly turning the brushes over in my hand.

Kathump.

Just then the walkie-talkie squealed. "Margot, we gotta go," came Baron's urgent voice. "Daddy didn't like the pot roast. He'd rather have Milton."

Kathump.

"I'll meet you at the front door. If I'm not there in thirty seconds make sure you leave it open," I called into the walkie.

"Ten-four."

At the tip of the green brush I spied aging flakes of red nail polish. Dirk's sister had used the polish to mark her brush.

Kathump.

I stuffed Dirk's blue toothbrush into my purse and quickly moved to the door. *Three-two-one.* I yanked it open just as Dirk's sister was about to make contact again. She came flying past me—well, flying for a zombie—into the bathroom, tripped, and fell into the tub.

I threw her toothbrush at her. "You need to use that more often," I called. Then I ran from the room. When I got to the bottom of the stairs I didn't see Dirk's daddy, but I could hear him. The front door hung wide open. As I raced down the hall past the den I heard Mrs. Conrad trying to calm her husband. I figured it wouldn't be long before she joined the rest of her family among the living dead. Her life of denial was coming to an end.

I exited, slamming the door. There. I'd finally met my boyfriend's family.

As we walked home, Baron and Milton were giddy with success.

"We did it, homie!" Milton called.

"The name's Chomsky. Baron Chomsky," Baron called back. They laughed and high-fived down the street.

"Hey. Let's sing a Christmas carol," Baron called.

"Why?" asked Milton.

"It's the holiday season, and I'm filled with the spirit. 'O come all ye faithful . . . ,'" he began. Within moments Milton joined him.

"'Joyful and triumphant . . .'"

Jubilant with their victory, their voices carried into the night. I kept an eye peeled. This was the kind of thing that could attract unwanted attention.

"Baron, you have a lovely voice," Sybil said when they finished. "It's kind of sexy."

"Really?" I'm sure that was the first time *sexy* had been used to describe anything Baron had ever done.

"Mmmm, yeah," she said in a voice smooth like velvet.

I gagged. *Could she be any more obvious?*

"Um . . . thanks." Baron was at a loss for words. He was the one who usually did the flirting. Being flirted with was brand-new for him.

"I think our voices complement each other. Let's do another one. I'm going to carol next to you for the rest of the night."

Baron looked at me. I pretended not to notice, keeping my eyes straight ahead.

"How about 'Silent Night'?" he asked. There was an uneasiness to his words.

Sybil sidled up next to him. "I love that one."

"Umm. Me too . . . Cute Stuff."

Cute Stuff?

And just like that, two years of pining for me were tossed out the window like dirty dishwater.

She grabbed his hand as we walked, *oohing* appropriately when he did his phony accent. I was embarrassed for her, pretending to be interested in the pathetic geek just to make me jealous. Sad.

"Umm, what's going on?" Milton asked. Baron and Sybil were halfway down the block. They had finished caroling, and he was demonstrating the zombie death grip he'd learned in the video game *Zombie Slayers*. "Did you and Baron have a fight or something?"

"No. Why would you say that?"

"I always thought you were Baron's girl."

"Please! Baron is just an annoying classmate. I have a boyfriend."

"Um. Okay." He thought for a second. "The antidote we've been working on is almost ready. Maybe you should rethink your relationship with Baron."

"Why's that?"

"Because we're about to be big shots around here. When we turn everyone back to normal we are going to be the big dogs."

"Really?"

"Yep." A beat and then, "Nothing against you, Margot. I think you're cool and all, but I'm going to take Amanda Culpepper to the prom."

I stared at him.

"I mean, how would it look, me going out with the girl my best friend just dumped? Now that I'm about to be The Man I have a reputation to uphold. Sorry."

Talk about delusional. The geeks had convinced themselves that turning everyone back to normal would catapult them to the top of the food chain. *Boy, are they in for a rude awakening.*

Speaking of rude awakenings, I was in the midst of one myself with Sybil. I couldn't believe she would mislead a poor, defenseless geek. How cruel.

We left Baron and Milton in front of the school. They were headed to their lab to work on the antidote. Sybil and I retreated to my bedroom, where we sipped hot chocolate. The only reason I allowed her to come back with me was to give her a piece of my mind.

"What do you think you're doing?"

"What do you mean?" she asked as she blew on her chocolate.

"Why are you flirting with Baron?"

"I like him." She plucked a dab of marshmallow from the chocolate and sucked it from her finger.

"No, you don't. Baron's a geek."

"Not to me." She sat on the edge of my bed and pretended to thumb through a fashion magazine.

"And he's *my* geek." I snatched the magazine from her hand. "Stop flirting with him!" I commanded.

"What do you care? You already have a boyfriend."

"I feel sorry for you." I shook my head sadly, as if she were the most pathetic thing on Earth.

"Do I detect a hint of jealousy?" There was a wry smile on her lips. I wanted to scratch it off.

"You're the one who's jealous."

"No, I'm happy for you *and* your boyfriend. Be happy for me. I think I found someone."

What could I say? She was obviously baiting me.

"Okay. If you want Baron he's yours. We'll have to double date sometime," I added sweetly.

"Yes. I hear there's a new zombie flick coming to the Cineplex. I'm sure Dirk will eat it up," she replied with equally sweet venom.

We smiled in each other's faces. There would be more to come.

Later that night, as I lay in bed, my mind drifted back over the evening's events: the trip to Dirk's house, meeting his mother, being attacked and nearly killed by his sister. But the event that played out over and over in my mind like something out of the movie *Groundhog Day* was Baron and Sybil holding hands and caroling down the street.

He called her "Cute Stuff." Hypocrite.

Without thinking, I got out of bed, opened my closet door,

and looked at myself in the mirror. Back in the eighth grade I'd had the mirror moved from the outside to the inside of the door so I wouldn't have to look into it all the time. I didn't enjoy mirrors the way I'm sure Amanda Culpepper did. They'd never been a great friend to me. But tonight I couldn't help myself.

I peered at myself in my shorts and tank top PJs. My fleshy arms, my large thighs. The tiniest ripple of fat peeked out from under the top. I sucked in my tummy and pulled the top down over it.

I imagined I saw the reflections of Sybil and Baron standing behind me, holding hands and singing "O Come All Ye Faithful" with great joy. She was rosy-cheeked and thin; even in her bulky winter overcoat she appeared svelte—no fleshy arms, no large thighs.

"Fools," I said out loud. "Beauty and the Geek. They deserve each other." With an angry chuckle, I closed the closet door and went back to bed. I could still hear them singing.

Sybil had gone strange on me. There was no other way to put it. Now that she had a *boyfriend* of her own she'd become distant. When we traveled around the school she wore a perpetual frown on her face. And the moment she was in the cafeteria it was as if she'd entered her own private domain.

Zombies were no longer allowed to sit with their cliques. She patrolled the cafeteria like a demon possessed, thumping her gum foil badge and forcing Goths to sit with emos, jocks with nerds.

"Keep it down over there," she called to me one day as she patrolled. I'd been laughing—not too loud, there were zombies around, but obviously too loud for Deputy Dawg. "What's so funny anyway?" she asked. Okay, I admit I was laughing at her. But I just couldn't get over how seriously she took her role of lunchroom monitor.

"Dirk just told the funniest joke," I said.

"Dirk is a zombie!" She practically spat the words at me.

"I know. That's what made it so funny. The punch line was *'Mmmmmmaaaargh!'* Hysterical." I laughed freely, pretending I was laughing at the ridiculous punch line. She rolled her eyes and zombie walked away.

On another day she brought her iPod docking station to school. She set the speakers up on a table at the front of the cafeteria. Then she put in her iPod and cranked the music all the way up. Tom Jones' "She's a Lady" filled the air.

The zombies were suddenly jarred from their stupor. They began growling and twitching. I got up and zombie walked over to her.

"What are you doing?"

"Adding a little joy to this gloomy lunchroom. Who can resist Tom Jones?" Sybil replied. She began swaying to the music.

"They can," I replied, pointing at the zombies, who were growling. They shook their heads and swatted at the air around them. I snatched Sybil's iPod from the docking station. The music abruptly stopped.

"What did you do that for?"

"They were going to attack us."

"No, they were not. They were enjoying themselves, unlike some people who seem to have forgotten how."

"Why are you trying to get under my skin? Isn't it enough that I let you have Baron?"

"You didn't *let* me have Baron. I took him!" she snarled.

Zombie attention in the cafeteria shifted to me and Sybil, arguing.

"Mmmmm." A stoner zombie rose from his seat and started in our direction.

"Put this in your purse and leave it there," I said, handing her back the iPod.

She looked around at the zombies rising from their seats, their attention on us. Then without a word she took the iPod and put it away.

It dawned on me then that Sybil was losing touch. I'd need to keep an eye on her before she destroyed my perfect semester.

"Mr. Pennyfield is on his way," Principal Taft said.

We were standing in the rear of the auditorium. The lights had been lowered and the seats were filled with zombie students—a feat unto itself.

The Holiday Pageant was usually the biggest event of the winter season. This year the Winter Dance would be the big event, but with Taft's supervisor set to attend, the pageant had to be special.

Taft fidgeted nervously. "How are we looking?" What he was really asking was, *When Pennyfield arrives are the zombies going to eat him?*

"Everything's fine, sir," I replied confidently, hoping my tone didn't betray my true feelings. "Keep him outside until the music begins. And both of you should stand by the door to get the full effect." What I was really saying was, *You should stand by the door in case you have to run.*

He nodded. "Yes. We don't want to miss the full effect."

A short time later, with Sybil, Baron, and Milton in place,

I lowered the house lights, turned up the stage lights, and pushed the button starting the music.

The opening strains of Michael Jackson's "Thriller" drifted into the auditorium. The curtain drew back as I slowly upped the stage lights on an eerie setting, a cemetery at Christmas. There was plastic snow on the floor, and wreaths on the cardboard headstones. Sybil and Baron appeared on stage, Baron doing an imitation of Michael Jackson mixed with a touch of James Bond—of course. They began acting out the "Thriller" video I'd found on YouTube.

With the dance number under way, I slipped from the control room and joined Taft and Mr. Pennyfield at the rear of the auditorium. Upon seeing Pennyfield the first thing I thought of was a mouse. He was small in stature, with twitchy features, and tiny eyes that wouldn't keep still.

"There she is," Taft said proudly as I walked up. "Mr. Pennyfield, meet Margot Johnson, the brains behind our little Christmas extravaganza."

I smiled and shook his hand, keeping a cautious eye on the activity onstage. Over in a corner stood Mrs. Mars. She smiled and nodded to us, but made no attempt to come over. I was surprised to see her there. Mrs. Mars didn't seem like the Holiday Pageant type.

A low moan drifted up from the sea of student onlookers.

"What's that?" asked Pennyfield, his eyes darting about.

"That's the way these kids show their appreciation," Taft said with a practiced chuckle. "*Mmmmm*," he mimicked. "It's the new hot thing. Don't they moan like that in all your schools?"

"Oh, yes. Yes, of course they do," Pennyfield replied, not wanting to appear out of touch. "Kids. It's so hard to keep up with them these days."

"Mmmm," I said, and smiled. Taft was playing him like a fiddle.

Onstage Baron and Sybil continued acting out the video. Now came the tough part. The monsters.

From the wings, zombies began shambling onto the stage.

"This is a rather odd song for the holidays," Pennyfield said suddenly.

Taft shot me a sideways glance. *Do something!*

"Well . . . ," I said, trying to buy some time. "I consider the holidays a perfect time to honor those who came before us."

"Ahh. So, those are spirits coming to greet the holiday revelers?" asked Pennyfield.

"Yup. You got it."

Pennyfield nodded appreciatively. Taft and I both breathed sighs of relief.

I glanced at the stage and imagined Baron, Sybil, and the zombies all doing the "Thriller" choreography matching the video step for step. In truth, Sybil and Baron were doing their best to stay out of the grasp of the slow-moving zombies.

The moaning from the audience grew louder and more intense. Then, suddenly and without warning, the zombies in the audience began to rise from their seats.

"What's happening?" whispered Taft as student zombies began making their way to the stage.

"Ms. Johnson!" Pennyfield said, his voice rising.

"Umm, I can explain, sir," I said as every zombie in the house made for Baron and Sybil.

He held up a finger, shushing me. "No, no. I understand completely. And . . . it's beautiful. The entire student body honoring those who have come before." His voice cracked with emotion. "Touching."

"That's it. Gotta go," I called as the zombies began to surround my friends.

"Yes. I have another school pageant to attend as well. But I'm so glad I got a chance to meet you, Ms. Johnson. This is the most inspiring Holiday Pageant ever. You have done your school proud."

Taft gave me a quick wink and hustled an emotional Pennyfield out. A moment later I was racing for the booth.

Onstage, Sybil and Baron were nearly surrounded. Their screams were real. They had stopped moving and were standing on top of the trapdoor to the pit, waiting for me to release it so they could drop to safety. I got to the booth and hit the button for the pit door as planned.

It didn't open.

I peered out the booth window at the stage below. A wave of nausea floated through my belly. Sybil and Baron were trapped.

The zombies shuffled toward them, extending their arms, fingers twitching with anticipation. They couldn't wait to have my friends join them among the living dead.

I wanted to run down to the stage and distract the zombies. But I knew by the time I got there it would be too late. I hit the button again and again, but nothing happened.

I slid the booth window open. "It's stuck!" I screamed down to them. "*Run!*"

I was wasting my voice. There was no place for them to run to.

The zombies stopped advancing, their eyes all moving to me in the safety of my little booth above the stage.

Just then Baron started jumping up and down.

Bounce—*crash!*

Over and over he landed hard on the stuck trapdoor. The sound brought the zombies' attention back to him and Sybil.

"Jump!" Baron called. Sybil didn't move. Her eyes rolled back into her head, and she fell to her knees. From the look of her it was game over.

Baron grabbed her hand. "Come on, we can do this, Sybil. Jump," he urged. The soft pleading of his voice must have cut through the fear that had clogged her brain, because she suddenly got up, filled with a berserk frenetic energy. Together they jumped up.

When Sybil jumped she pitched her arms up into the air, her legs splayed wide, as if throwing every ounce of fight left in her into it. As serious as the situation was, her spastic movements were hilarious.

Crash! When they landed the trapdoor gave way with a thunderous crack. Just as the zombies reached them, Baron and Sybil fell through to the pit below, and then the door slammed shut.

The zombies onstage staggered in herky-jerky circles, trying to figure out what had become of their prey. I slumped back in my chair and heaved a huge sigh. Yet instead of waves of relief washing over me, I realized I'd been smiling, chuckling.

Oh, my God! Stop it! I thought. *This is nothing to laugh about.* I told myself the chuckling was because of Sybil's spastic movements. . . . I hoped that was true.

It was then I heard Sybil scream.

Sybil's screams propelled me down to the basement and up to the door leading to the pit. When I entered, Sybil was sitting across the cramped room on an old wooden stool. She was alternately sobbing and screaming. Baron was crouched by her side, attempting to console her.

Milton was by the door looking on. "She seemed okay at first, and then all of a sudden she started freaking out."

"I . . . could . . . have . . . Ahhhhh!" Sybil wailed. Baron patted her hand, and spoke to her in a soothing tone.

"I guess when it sank in that she was this close to becoming one of them . . ." Milton's words trailed off. "My diagnosis is it's a mild case of hysteria. She'll be okay." He moved away.

"It's all right, Sybil. We're fine now," said Baron. There was concern in his voice. "I wouldn't have let anything happen to you." She sniffled and nodded. She was calming now. Baron continued to pat her hand.

At that moment a rush of jealousy surged through me like a shot of adrenaline. This was a side of Baron I hadn't seen before—or hadn't taken the time to notice. Baron had been calm and resourceful in saving their lives, and now he was comforting Sybil. It was the kind of gallant thing I would have expected from . . . Dirk.

I should have rushed to my friend's side and thrown my arms around her. But seeing her being comforted by Baron, I couldn't. . . . I just couldn't.

"Well, it looks like everything's okay here. I think I should go check on Dirk. Great job, guys."

It was only then that Sybil realized I was in the room. She looked up at me, still sniffling, her eyes narrowed. "Where did you say you were going?"

"Dirk. I just want to check on him. I'll be back."

Her red-rimmed eyes seared into me.

"Dirk!" she cried, her voice crackling. "We could have died at the hands of zombies and you want to go check on one of them?"

"Technically, they're not zombies," Milton called. "They're victims of a viral infection that seems to affect the entire frontal lobe—"

"Not now, Milton," said Baron.

"I'm just saying, zombies want to eat your brains out. All these guys want to do is kill you."

Sybil's eyes were still on me.

"Well . . . you didn't die," I said in a dismissive tone. "Baron saved you."

"We saved each other." His voice was soft and soothing as he massaged Sybil's shoulder.

She stared at me in silence. The look in her eyes was unnerving. I'd never seen anything like it from her before. It was a look of . . . disgust.

"See here," called Milton. He was holding two plywood slats with nails sticking out of them. "Someone nailed it shut."

He pointed with one of the slats, and we looked up to the ceiling, where the remaining plywood slats that had kept the pit door from opening now hung ready to collapse.

"Well, would you look at that," I said, my voice sounding unnatural.

"My diagnosis, someone did this on purpose." Milton turned to Baron. "I told you, homie. We are not alone."

"Let's not jump to any conclusions. It could have been nailed shut from before," I said weakly. "Who knows? Maybe it's been nailed shut since last year."

"You didn't test it?" Sybil's eyes raged at me. Her stare was like a blowtorch against my flesh. I had to get away.

"No," I said. "I . . . didn't. I'm sorry."

"She didn't do it on purpose," Baron said, coming to my defense. "She's had a lot on her mind with the pageant and everything." He looked at me. "I knew you'd pull it off." There was empathy in his soft, hazel eyes. I looked at Sybil. Hers were filled with fury.

"We must be getting close," Milton said. "Someone is really trying to stop us."

"I need to find Dirk. If what you say is true he may be in danger." It was a weak excuse, but I had to say something, anything, to get away from Sybil's accusing gaze. I turned to go.

"Trust no one," Milton called as I exited.

"Yes," I heard Sybil say as the door closed behind me. "Trust no one."

My mind was a jumble of emotion as I headed away from the pit room. I did not try to clear it. As long as my thoughts were jammed together into a ball of emotional Silly Putty, I didn't have to think. Thinking meant facing myself, and that, I was sure, was an ugly proposition. So I cruised down the corridor, my mind a total blur.

The basement corridor was dimly lit. It had been an eerie place even before the zombies arrived. Since their arrival it was like something straight out of a horror flick. Suddenly I stopped, my heart pounding. Four zombie girls were standing in the shadows at the end of the corridor.

They were at least a hundred feet away. If I had to, I knew I could escape by going back in the direction I'd come. No problem.

I calmed myself.

"Mmmmuh." Upon seeing me, a soft moan escaped one of the girls. She stepped toward me, emerging from the shadows. It was Amanda. Her yellow sundress was even more rumpled and frayed than before. This creature was a far cry from the fastidious Amanda we'd all come to know and hate.

The four it-girl zombies smoothed their rumpled clothes, their dark eyes never leaving me.

Are they going to attack?

I took a halting step backward, peering into the Amanda thing's eyes. They seemed awash with indifference.

Then she began to move—not toward me, but away from me.

The Zombiettes instinctively shambled after her.

"Where are you going?" I heard myself call. The emotion I'd been keeping bottled up inside cascaded out of me. "You're never going to get to be anything around here ever again unless you bite me!"

The zombies disappeared around the bend in the corner.

I rushed to the corner and stepped around. The four zombie girls were shuffling away. "You hear me, Amanda? I'm the popular one now. Your reign is over unless you bite me!" Propelled by emotion, I took a few steps after them. "What are you so afraid of? *Bite me!*" I screamed. They didn't stop or look back. They continued moving away, and in a few moments they were gone.

Alone in the corridor, I crumpled to the floor, tears streaming down my cheeks. The snub from Amanda had caught me off guard. But one thing became clear—I was still a zero in her zombie eyes, just as I'd been since the eighth grade. "Bite me," I rasped.

Chapter

Twenty-four

 At home that evening, I sat on the edge of my bed staring at the walls, the Holiday Pageant playing over in my mind like a horrible dream. I could still see Baron and Sybil scrambling, could still hear their screams. It wasn't funny now. It was tragic. Someone had tried to kill my best friend.

Perhaps my laughter had been some sort of defense mechanism for handling pain, I told myself. Yes, that was it! I wasn't chuckling over my friend's near demise; I was dealing with the pain of her near-death experience.

My thoughts moved to the room beneath the pit, where I could still see Baron comforting her.

Well, why wouldn't he comfort her? Stupid fools nearly got themselves killed. They deserve each other.

A tiny smile appeared on my lips.

Stop it! That's not funny.

Yes, it is. Can you imagine geeky Baron actually being somebody's boyfriend? Who'd want him? And you definitely don't need a geek like him comforting you.

I don't?

Of course not. Your boyfriend is the cutest, most popular boy in school—Dirk Conrad. Now all you have to do is keep your mind on the manifesto—chairman of all the important committees, a boyfriend, popularity. That's what's important. You should be glad that the Amanda zombie didn't bite you. You're better than her.

I *was* the most popular girl at Salesian High. Forget about Sybil, Baron, and Amanda. I didn't need any of them. My thoughts found solace in the dark place.

I went to the living room, where Dirk was watching reruns of *Fear Factor* with my parents. He was sitting on the couch next to my father, a takeout box of ribs between them.

"Is everything all right, dear?" my mother asked.

"Yes. Dirk and I just need to practice for our big dance, in case I'm crowned winter queen next Friday night."

"Your father and I are so proud of you," my mother said. Her words caught me off guard.

"Umm, thanks."

"You're so popular all of a sudden. Your father and I always knew you would be. You're an amazing young lady."

"You think I'm . . . amazing?" A small smile appeared on my lips.

She looked at me as if my question was totally ridiculous. "Are you *sure* you're all right?"

"Yeah." Then I said, "Mom, what was it like when you were in high school?"

She shook her head and laughed. "I wouldn't wish for that again."

"Why not?"

She thought about it a moment. "I wasn't popular like you when I was in high school. Look at you—running for queen of the Winter Dance. And I didn't have a good friend like Sybil, and a boyfriend . . ." She laughed as if it was a ridiculous notion. "I wasn't sure of myself, like you are. High school for me was not fun."

In that moment I felt as though I was living a lie. I dismissed the thought.

"You're having a great time in high school, and we're happy for that. Just remember what's important, dear."

And now, yet another brief note to parents: Stop being so cryptic with your advice to us. "Keep your head on straight." "Remember what's important." If our response to your words of wisdom is a smile and a nod, we have no idea what you're talking about.

I smiled and nodded.

"Ooh, look, they're eating giant beetles," she called, pointing to the TV. Her attention shifted back to the show.

I took Dirk by the hand and led him away.

"Leave your door open!" my father called.

Back in my room, I attempted to get Dirk to take me in his arms. He tried to bite me.

"Listen to me, Dirk," I said, stepping away. "I know these past weeks together must mean something to you. And that beneath the zombie haze that's fogged up your brain, you really care for me. So I need for you to concentrate right now. Okay?"

I thought of my mother's words: "I wasn't popular like you when I was in high school."

"Just imagine you and me, the king and queen of the Winter Dance, dancing across the gymnasium floor, with the entire student body—Amanda, Sybil, Baron—all looking on. The most popular kids at school—*us*. Wouldn't that be fabulous?"

"Mmmm."

Was that a grunt of recognition? Am I getting through to him?

"Okay. Then we have to do this." I inched closer and gingerly placed myself in his arms. "That's it," I said softly. I began to hum "Wonderful Tonight." It was the perfect song for a queen's dance.

Dirk folded me into his arms, allowing me to lead him awkwardly into a dance. We bumped into my desk, the dresser, my bed, but we were dancing. I closed my eyes, and was whisked away to the Winter Dance, gliding gracefully across the floor, every jealous eye in the house on me, while Eric Clapton captured my feelings so perfectly, singing of the beautiful lady on his arm who looked wonderful tonight.

Dirk's grip tightened.

"Ease up, Dirk, you're hurting me."

"Mmmmmahhh!" His lips parted and began moving toward my shoulder.

"No, Dirk! Concentrate!"

His arms were like vise grips, squeezing tighter and tighter. I struggled in his grasp, but he was too strong. There was no way I could escape. Saliva drizzled from his hungry lips, onto my shoulder and down my arm. I pulled the newspaper from my waistband, and swatted him across the nose.

"Yeeeeee!" His head snapped back instantly. He released me and retreated across the room, cowering onto my bed.

I looked at Dirk, saw the fear in his crimson eyes.

Is this the boyfriend I'd dreamed of all through junior high?

Tears welled up in my eyes as thoughts of Baron and Sybil holding hands, Amanda and her Twigettes rejecting me, fired through. I was the most popular girl at school, and yet I felt invisible.

"We'll show them." My lips were trembling.

I pulled a few meat scraps from the Baggie on my desk. Then I moved to the bed and held my arms open wide. "Come, darling," I called softly. "Let's try it again."

Chapter
Twenty-five

 The following evening, Dirk and I were back in my room. It was a little less than a week away from the Winter Dance, and I was determined to have him hold me in his arms.

It wasn't love that drove me. I was fueled by the darkness in my soul. All the darkness wanted to do was win, achieve my manifesto, and thumb my nose at those who'd doubted me.

Nyah, nyah, nyah, nyah, nyah—look at what I did!

In an attempt to cheer myself up I pulled out the manifesto:

I, Margot Jean Johnson, being of sound mind and in front of my best friend, Sybil Mulcahy, and the entire world, hereby decree that my high school experience will far exceed that of junior high.

"Yes," I said, pumping my fist into the air. I expected a delicious satisfaction to course through me.

Instead, I felt nothing.

I will be popular . . .

"Yes, again." I was the Salesian High it-girl. And so what if there were only two living girls in the entire school. *I* was the chairman of the Yearbook Committee; *I* was the chairman of the Winter Dance Committee; *I* set the trends; *I* called the shots. *Me, me, me, me, me!* I was the queen bee.

I will be invited to parties . . .

"Yes, once again." The Winter Dance would be the social event of the year, maybe even the decade. I made out the guest list so Amanda Culpepper and the undead heads were persona non grata.

With all this good news, shouldn't I be dancing on the ceiling? Instead, I was feeling worse.

I will have a boyfriend . . .

I looked over at Dirk and was bathed in a certain dread. It came as a cold clamminess chilling me to my bones.

"Are you worth it?" I asked. I had sacrificed my ethics, my friends, myself to achieve . . . what?

Of course he's worth it. By the end of the semester you will have realized every high school goal you ever set for yourself.

Despite nearly achieving all my dreams, there was a part of me that realized it was all a sham. This was the truth I'd been avoiding, the reason for the tears in my eyes. I put the manifesto away.

"Margot! Some guys outside want to talk to you," Theo called down the hall.

I went to the front door and found Baron and Milton bundled up against the cold on my porch, smiles as big as the Grand Canyon on both their faces.

"Guess what?" asked Milton.

"Milton, I'm busy." I had no time for geek enthusiasm.

"So were we." He pulled a small vial from his pocket and held it out to me. He could hardly contain himself. "Wanna know what's in it? Wanna know, wanna know?"

"Okay, I'll bite. What's in it?"

"The answer to our prayers," he chimed. Then he and Baron giggled like a couple of schoolgirls. "Go on. Take it," he said.

I took the tiny vial. Inside, there was a luminescent, milky white liquid. "The antidote?" I asked.

"Yes, yes, yes!" He spun around like a whirling dervish. "This time next semester me and my homie here will be the two most popular guys at Salesian. Told you!" The two boys slapped a lame high-five.

"Where's Sybil?" I suddenly asked. "I'm surprised the three of you aren't out on the town celebrating this wonderful occasion." I hoped I didn't sound like a jealous child.

"Sybil hasn't been doing too well since the pageant," Baron said. There was genuine concern on his face. "She's home resting."

"Oh." A twinge of shame rode through me. "Well . . . congratulations," I said flatly. I handed back the vial.

"No, no. You have to give it to Dirk. He's our guinea pig," said Milton.

"I'm not giving this to Dirk. I don't even know what's in it."

"But you have to!" squawked Milton.

"Yeah. The antidote only works if it's ingested by a zombie," Baron added. "We figured you'd want to be first."

"Why would I want to be first?"

"I knew it!" Milton thrust an accusing finger at me. "You don't want him to change back."

"Chill, dude." Baron looked me in the eye and lowered his voice. "Can we talk?"

I stepped out onto the porch, and Baron walked me a few feet away from an agitated Milton. "Margot, you gotta do this. Our classmates are all zombies. I know you know that isn't right."

"Why me?"

"You're the only one who can get close enough. Your . . . boyfriend . . . is a zombie." The word *boyfriend* seemed to stick in his throat.

"But what if it hurts him?"

"Margot, he's a zombie. I don't think his life can get much worse." He leaned in. "But think of what it will mean if it does work. When Dirk realizes you're the one who changed him back, he'll be yours forever."

Did I sense a note of sadness in his voice when he said that?

I looked into his hazel eyes. When I'd helped with getting the DNA, I hadn't believed they could pull it off. The self-assured boy standing before me was a far cry from the geek he was back then. These past several weeks Baron had transformed into the cool, suave image he'd always tried to project. Or was it me who had changed?

"I can see why Sybil likes you so much," I said.

His eyes widened for an instant. "What's that supposed to mean?"

"I don't know." I sighed. "I guess if this works we'll both get what we want, huh?" I'm not sure why I said it, but I was anxious to hear what his response would be.

"I guess," he replied.

Not what I was looking for.

I stared down at the vial in my hand. It was suddenly hot and heavy. "Okay, I'll do it," I said, quickly stuffing it into my pocket. I shot him a small smile. "Let's hope for the best."

"Yeah," he said. "Let's hope for the best."

There was a hint of sadness on his face as he and Milton turned and walked away.

When I got back to my room, I discovered Dirk working himself into a frenzy, chasing and then trapping a spider. He caught the insect and wolfed it down as if it were a delicacy. Then it was like the shades had gone down in his eyes. Nobody home.

Baron was right. Dirk's life couldn't get much worse. I had the power to put an end to this.

A wave of relief washed over me, like a soothing lotion. For the first time in a long time, I had a chance to feel good about myself. I had the power to put an end to all my classmates' misery. Maybe Baron and Milton were right. Maybe I'd be a hero for helping save the day.

I went to my closet, pulled out my hip-hugger jeans and another of the sexy tops my father hated. Then I went to the bathroom and changed. This is how I wanted Dirk to see me when he got back to being himself.

I came back into my room, picked up the vial, removed the stopper, and poured the luminescent liquid over several hunks of raw meat I always kept handy for Dirk's visits. I picked up a sliver of the coated meat. Dirk eyed me attentively, waiting for me to throw the meat as I'd done in the past.

"Well, boyfriend, in a few minutes you just might be your old self again," I said brightly.

I conjured up images of the old Dirk Conrad, his smile, his

glacier blues that gave every girl at school a loin-ache. At that moment the image of Dirk and Amanda's photo button from the carnival ignited in my thoughts.

See how happy he is with me? He'll never be that happy with you.

It was then I remembered another Dirk Conrad, the one who hadn't wanted to go to the carnival with me, the one who was dating Amanda Culpepper. I gazed at the new Dirk, who was waiting patiently for a piece of raw meat. The new Dirk didn't care that I wasn't skinny as a rail. The new Dirk came to my house every night, and sat on my bed while I did my homework, and then watched reruns of *Law & Order* with my parents.

The new Dirk was perfect.

I wouldn't—I couldn't—give him back to Amanda Culpepper.

"You don't mind remaining a zombie, do you?" My voice cracked with self-hatred. "No sense getting your hopes up, anyway. This stuff probably doesn't even work. Face it, the geeks made it." I snatched up a piece of meat that hadn't been dipped in the antidote and threw it to him. As he gobbled it down, I ran into the bathroom, then flushed the treated meat.

Chapter

Twenty-six

 I carried the weight of my cowardly deed (or undeed, since I hadn't actually *done* anything) into the final week of school before winter break. I went to class among the zombies each day, my head filled with justifications.

It's just till after the Winter Dance; then I'll see to it that Dirk gets the antidote.

I dodged Baron and Milton at school, and told Theo to tell them I wasn't home if they stopped by.

After school, I went to the gym, where I continued hanging decorations for the Winter Dance. I had chosen an eighties theme around the song "Let the Music Play." The idea being we would all throw our cares in the air and dance the night away. Big whoop. It was a cheesy idea, but it was the best I could come up with alone. And with no one around to challenge it, the idea stood.

When I'd begun the decorating process a few weeks ago, Sybil had been by my side, working joyously. But no more. Now, whenever I saw Sybil in class she shot me the same accusing stare she'd treated me to after the Holiday Pageant in the pit room.

My guilt was mounting. It had worked its way under my skin. Like a tick it burrowed into my flesh, creating an itch I couldn't scratch. I missed Sybil. I wanted to tell her how badly I was feeling about what I'd done. But my pride wouldn't let me. So I avoided her at all costs.

Tuesday was the state endurance exam. When I walked into the gym, Mrs. Mars was waiting for me by the door.

"Margot Jean Johnson, good morning. Well, today's the big day."

"I know. And I'd love to take the exam with the rest of the class, but I've been experiencing trouble keeping my balance lately." I weaved from side to side as I handed her my note:

Dear Mrs. Mars,
Please excuse our intrepid daughter, Margot, from
participating in the state endurance exam today. Last night
she sat too close to the TV and I'm afraid it affected her
equilibrium. We fear she may fall doing all that running
and climbing, and seriously injure herself. Feel free to give
her a written version of the exam.

Sincerely,
Mrs. Trudi Johnson

"Written version of the exam? Interesting."

"That would solve everything," I said.

"Margot, I know you think you're getting over. But did you ever think that maybe the only person you're getting over on is you?"

"I don't know what you're talking about, Mrs. Mars, but I really need to get into the bleachers. I'm about to fall down here."

A somber look came over her. It was a look I hadn't seen before. "All right, but before I fail you and you have to repeat next semester, why don't you stop by my office later in the day and have a little chat?"

"Umm. Okay."

It was sounding like she might pass me just for talking with her later in the day. I wouldn't even have to take a written test. With the world falling down around me, I was finally getting some good news. Mrs. Mars knew running, jumping, and climbing added no value to our lives. She was finally getting real.

When I left the gym, my day took a turn for the worse.

"Where have you been?" Baron and Milton were standing outside my French classroom door.

"Around. Now, if you'll excuse me . . ." I attempted to brush by them. They blocked my path.

"We've been calling you. We even stopped by your house," said Baron. He was trying to act cool, but they were both upset.

"Oh?"

"You didn't give it to him, did you?" accused Milton. "I knew it!"

"For your information, I did give it to him."

"And?" Their faces filled with little-boy expectation.

"And it didn't work."

"*Liar!*" screamed Milton, pounding his fists against his thighs.

A few zombies in the corridor emerged from their daze, focusing their attention on us.

"We need to reconvene," Baron said softly. "Zombie walk to the boys' bathroom."

Together we shuffled away from the zombies and into the—yech!—boys' bathroom.

What a mess.

Sheets of wet toilet paper were strewn across the floor as if a madman had decided to carpet the place with it. There were large puddles in front of each urinal. I don't even want to imagine how they got there. Chicken-scratch graffiti covered the walls. I will not waste my time repeating the childish comments written there.

"It smells in here," I said, pinching shut my nose.

"It's a bathroom."

"The girls' bathroom doesn't smell like this."

"What does it smell like?"

"Not this!"

"*Liar!*" Milton screeched again. He stamped his feet like a petulant child.

"What did you call me?" I clenched my fists, enraged.

"Why don't you just tell us the truth, Margot? You didn't give it to him," he accused.

"For your information, I did give it to him." The lie flew from my lips too quickly. Even I was unconvinced.

"I don't believe her," Milton squawked at Baron. "I don't believe you," he squawked at me. "Show me the empty vial." His doubting eyes challenged me.

I calmed myself and reached into my bag, where I produced the now-empty vial. Just the residue of the remaining antidote coated the bottom.

Baron took the vial from my hand and looked me in the eye. "You really gave it to him?"

I nodded.

His face filled with despair. "I . . . don't . . . believe it," he stammered. "We were so sure it would work."

I couldn't get over how easily they trusted me. But Milton took his lead from Baron, and Baron didn't want to believe I was a liar. Both boys slumped against the wall, their heads sagging as their hopes for high school popularity faded.

"I'm sorry," I said, grateful the interrogation was over.

"How did you give it to him?" asked Milton. The antagonism had gone out of him.

"I dipped some slivers of raw steak in it. I watched him eat them. You didn't tell me how long it was supposed to take, but after a day I realized it hadn't worked."

"That's impossible," Milton said to no one. He mumbled the formula to himself over and over.

"Wow. Tough blow." Baron looked thoughtful. "Well, I guess we need to rethink the formula. Thanks for trying it out for us." He smiled bravely. I had to admire his resilience.

"We'll be back," he said. It was supposed to sound like Arnold Schwarzenegger. It didn't.

I watched them exit the bathroom, their heads hanging low, two little boys lost in the woods. I promised myself I would tell them the truth right after the Winter Dance.

A short time later I was back in the gym, high up on a ladder, hanging giant foil snowflakes along with large black musical notes for the Winter Dance. The disappointment in Baron's eyes when I had lied to him about the antidote kept running through my mind. They were gorgeous eyes. I didn't like seeing pain in them—especially pain caused by me.

I tried again to justify to myself why it was perfectly all right not to use the antidote. But my house of cards was falling down. Even the voice inside me was running out of plausible lies. I was like an addict who knew she should stop using yet continued to use every day. Like an addict, I knew my lies were destroying my entire universe. A part of me thought maybe I deserved it.

Just then, someone tapped on the ladder. I stiffened, and looked down into the chastising eyes of Sybil Mulcahy.

"Can I have a word with you, please?" she called up. Her voice was very official.

"Can it wait till after school, or will you be hanging out with your *boyfriend*?"

She stomped her foot. "Margot, get down here, now!"

"What are you getting so huffy about?"

"Margot Jean Johnson, you know good and well what I'm getting huffy about, and if we ever meant anything to each other, we need to talk about it."

She called me by my full name. Not the way Mrs. Mars did, but the way her mother did when she was angry with her. "Sybil Joyce Mulcahy!" her mother would yell. That always got Sybil. Now she was doing it to me.

"Oh, all right," I said. I started down the ladder. "I'd be finished with these decorations already if you hadn't bailed on me." I reached the bottom and smoothed my clothing, trying to act nonchalant. In truth, my heart was racing a mile a minute. I'd been dreading this moment for days.

"Margot, this Winter Dance is a joke."

"It's not a joke!" My defenses went up like the forcefield around the starship *Enterprise*. "It's the culmination of a most excellent semester."

"Excellent semester?" Her voice rose with agitation. "You have a boyfriend who wants to kill you, classmates who want to kill you, and because of you, they almost killed *me*!"

"I didn't say it was perfect."

"Margot, I know you weren't thinking straight when you nailed shut the trapdoor, but—"

"Are you accusing me of nailing shut the trapdoor?" Her hurtful words slammed into my heart. I'd done a lot of things to Sybil these past six weeks, but I'd never tried to kill her.

She stared at me long and hard, the accusation scrawled across her face. "Yes. I am."

Just then the lights went out.

The entire gym was suddenly dark as pitch. I could no longer see Sybil. I couldn't see my own hand.

"I guess we blew a fuse," I said, trying to make light of the moment.

Clunk. The outside door swung open, and light from the corridor spilled in. A shadowy person backlit by the fluorescent lights in the corridor heaved something toward the center of the gym, and then slammed the door shut. The weighty thing landed with a thud, echoing throughout the gym.

"You smell roast beef?" Sybil asked.

A low moaning sprang up in the darkness from over by the locker room door. "Mmmmm."

Swish-swish. The deliberate shuffle of slow feet. The footsteps were moving toward us. *Swish-swish, swish-swish.* More moaning, more feet.

"What's that?" whispered Sybil, fear creeping into her voice.

"I don't know," I said. But we both knew exactly what it was. Zombies had smelled the meat, and were pouring in from the locker room.

"We need to get out of here." Her words were panic-stricken. She'd already been through a horrible ordeal, and here it was happening all over again. "We need to get out of here!" she repeated, as she attempted to exert some control over the situation.

"No," I said. I reached through the darkness and found her arm. "We need to stay put."

Swish-swish.

If we'd gone for the door, I was certain we would have found it locked. Just as I was certain the person who threw the slab of roast beef was the same person who had let the zombies in. This was no blackout, no high school prank, no mistake. Somebody wanted us dead . . . or undead.

Swish-swish.

"Who's out there?" Sybil cried out with fake bravado. But the fear that colored her words told me she was going to pieces.

Swish-swish. Closer now.

"Sybil?" I said, hoping she hadn't totally checked out.

"Huh?" Her voice was small and weak. It was the voice of defeat.

"Listen to me. I need your lucky flashlight."

"What?"

"The flashlight I gave you for your birthday. You always have it with you. I need you to get it out. And hurry!"

"Mmmmm. Grrowl!" Through the darkness we could hear that the zombies had reached the roast beef, and were fighting over it. The only thing keeping us from being torn to shreds was the cloak of darkness—and our silence.

"*Please!*" I cried.

The zombies stopped fighting.

Definitely not good. The sudden stillness told me they were slowly refocusing their attention in our direction.

"Mmmmm." *Swish-swish.* Their labored movement shifted in the darkness. They were coming for us.

"Sybil Joyce Mulcahy, I need that flashlight," I said, channeling her mother. "And I need it now!"

That jarred her out of her fugue. I could hear her fumbling in her purse. "Here it is." Her voice was even weaker than before.

I reached out and found her hand. "Sybil, I need you to pay attention and do exactly as I say. Okay?"

"Ouch!" she cried. "What was that?"

"*Sybil Joyce Mulcahy!*" I screamed again. "You need to pay

attention! When I say 'now,' shine the flashlight on me, casting my shadow on the wall. Got it?"

"Got it," she said. But I could tell she'd lost all hope of getting out alive.

Quickly, I pulled my hair back into a tight bun, cinching it with a scrunchie.

Swish-swish. The zombies were on top of us. I could feel them reaching for us, bony fingers finding my arms in the darkness.

"*Now!*"

Click. The tiny light beam hit me from the side, casting my huge, distorted profile onto the wall.

"Margot Jean Johnson," I said in a throaty voice I prayed would sound like Mrs. Mars. "I want you and all of your friends out of this gym. And if you're not out of here when the lights come back on, you will *all* be in my class next semester. Same bat time, same bat channel." I ended with a throaty chuckle and held my breath. Sybil clicked the penlight off on cue as if we'd planned it, again bathing the gym in darkness.

We waited in silence for a moment that stood still, and then . . . *swish-swish, swish-swish.* Zombie footsteps began moving quickly away from us toward the locker room door. *Swish-swish, swish-swish. Swish-swish, swish-swish.* The zombies continued their retreat. In a few minutes we were alone in the darkness, surrounded by welcome silence.

The lights came back on.

The empty gym was eerily silent. A bloody wet spot on the floor marked where the slab of meat had landed. The meat was gone. All I could think was, *That could have been us.*

"Someone is trying to kill us." Sybil's distant voice broke the silence.

I looked at her, my mind racing in a million different directions. All I could say was, "Yes. I wonder who." The words trembled from my lips.

We decided to ditch seventh period and hung out in the "up" stairwell between the second and third floors. We sat silently on the stairs, listening to each other breathe. The sound of our breathing calmed us—in and out, slow and steady. It was life-affirming.

"I'm sorry I accused you of nailing shut the pit door. I knew you couldn't have done it. It's just that—"

I held up my hand and stopped her. I had been guilty of so much, I understood why.

"I think it's Principal Taft," she said after a while. "He knew we were going to be in the gym."

It was then I noticed tributaries of bright red snaking through the whites of her eyes. Her pupils were dilated.

"You don't look too good."

"I know. I'm not feeling too good. I think it's all the excitement." She put her hand to her forehead. "I think I'm getting a fever."

I gasped.

On the back of Sybil's hand, between her thumb and forefinger, there was a half-moon bite mark, and a tiny trace of blood.

"Oh my God," I said, the fear rising in me like a tidal wave. "Sybil, what's that?"

Sybil looked at her hand. It was a childlike examination, filled with wonder. She turned it over several times, examining it from every angle. "Oh? That's what I felt in the darkness." She looked at me, and spoke calmly. "I guess when we were in the gym, one of the zombies bit me."

 The world I had created was crumbling all around me. I didn't have far to look to know whose fault it was. Sybil was becoming a zombie. Dark circles had formed under her eyes—eyes that were slowly becoming a sea of red.

"I think it's Principal Taft," she said again. "Or maybe it's Mrs. Mars. You're the only person in class she can't control. Turning you into a zombie would put you under her thumb like the others."

"Sybil, we've got to do something about that bite!" I couldn't think about who might have caused the attack, not with her life slipping slowly away. "We may not have much time. Remember what Principal Taft said about the carnival? They started changing right away."

"I know," she said softly. She sat there calmly, but I could smell the fear on her, like the stink of cheesy tennis shoes stinging in my nose . . . or perhaps it was my own fear I smelled.

Cough.

"What was that?" Sybil whispered, looking around.

My breath caught in my throat as I recognized the odor stinging my nose. I'd smelled it before.

I put a finger to my lips, signaling for silence, and then pointed to the landing below us. "Someone's listening," I whispered.

There was a slight rustling of clothing from the landing below.

"Whoever it is has all the answers." I grabbed Sybil's hand.

"What are you doing?"

I didn't respond. Silently, I pulled her downstairs. As quiet as we were, with every step we could hear the person retreating.

"He's on to us," I said. "Let's go!"

We bolted down the stairs two at a time, but the person we were chasing was doing the same. The culprit hit the first-floor landing and shot through the swinging door—*swoosh*. We arrived seconds later and barreled through into the first-floor corridor. Silence. Empty. We looked up and down the corridor. Nothing.

"He got away," Sybil said, catching her breath.

"Or maybe it was *she* who got away."

Sybil slid to the floor. "I'm so tired."

"Rest," I said. She looked horrible. It was as if she'd aged ten years right before my eyes. But at least she wasn't a zombie . . . yet.

That's when I saw it. In their retreat, the person's clothing had caught on a tiny nail sticking out of the door. A small piece of fabric now clung to the nail. "Look," I called.

I removed the tiny swatch from the nail. We examined it closely under the light. I rubbed the silky blue swatch between my thumb and forefinger, getting a feel for the soft material. I'd seen the fabric somewhere before. But where? I couldn't remember, but I knew I had to. My best friend's survival might well depend on deciphering the tiny clue.

I turned to Sybil, slumped on the floor. Her complexion had turned ghastly pale. "Let me see the bite."

"Margot, it's nothing. It doesn't even hurt."

"I need to see how bad it is." I grabbed her hand and examined it. There were two tiny puncture wounds. "The thing's teeth didn't break much flesh. Maybe only a tiny bit of the virus got in. Maybe this is the worst of it."

She nodded. "I am feeling a bit better."

"Maybe I should try sucking it out."

She drew back her hand. "You mean like snake venom?"

"Yes. We might be able to limit the damage if I suck it out." She smiled.

"What?"

"I knew the real Margot was in there somewhere." Her smile broadened. I looked away. The smile was as bad as her accusing stare. Same effect—heavy guilt.

"Give me your hand, Syb," I said, avoiding her eyes.

She shook her head. "You know I can't let you suck on my wound. It's too dangerous. Someone has to be around to end this thing."

Just my luck that someone would be me, the person who'd caused all this misery in the first place. "The boys," I said all of a sudden. "Maybe they have some of the antidote left." My voice rose with hope.

"They finished the antidote?"

"Um . . . Yes. Baron didn't tell you?"

"No."

I couldn't tell if not knowing had hurt her. She was so out of it.

"Umm . . . He probably didn't tell you because he gave me

some to give to Dirk and it didn't work," I said, trying to justify Baron's silence.

"Oh," she said softly. "But if it didn't work, what good would it do now?"

"Well . . . Maybe it just didn't work on Dirk. Maybe it'll work on you."

"No offense, Margot, but I wouldn't put much faith in a failed antidote." She was smiling again. "Although I appreciate your optimism."

"We have to try something!" My words reeked of desperation.

She nodded and heaved a deep sigh. "I guess we do." She shrugged. "Okay. Let's go."

School was out by the time we reached the basement. The zombie students had all vacated the premises. Walking the halls with Sybil made the dimly lit basement seem even creepier. Her breath came in short, ragged bursts, punctuating the silence around us. *She's beginning to sound like one of them,* I thought. I quickened my pace.

Up ahead we saw the handwritten cardboard sign declaring THE FORTRESS OF SOLITUDE hanging on the door. I was flooded with relief.

We entered. The room was empty . . . abandoned was more like it. Baron and Milton's hideout, which had once contained lab equipment and youthful optimism, now appeared to have been ransacked. A prickly feeling spread over my entire body, as if someone were sticking me with hundreds of tiny needles.

"They're not here." My eyes darted around the room. "This cannot be happening." Hurriedly, I began rummaging through the dusty bins and cubbies, hoping to find the antidote. Nothing.

Sybil seated herself on a lab stool, watching me go through

my search. I glanced over at her a few times. She appeared to be resigned to her fate.

"Someone got to them," she said. These were words I didn't want to hear, couldn't accept.

"I bet they went into deep hiding. You know, until they could fix the formula. You know how secretive Milton can get." My mind raced, searching for a plausible reason as to why they weren't here.

She shook her head. "Looks like there was a struggle."

She was right. It appeared more than a hasty retreat. It appeared forced.

"Someone got to them," she repeated.

So much for plausibility. We were silent for what seemed like forever. I could hear the sound of our hearts beating, hers with a slow, rhythmic pulse, mine racing like the wind.

"You need to stay away from me. Who knows when the change will come? When it does, I may try to kill you."

"You wouldn't," I said, my voice cracking. "Even as a zombie, I know you wouldn't."

"Don't be so sure. Dirk tried to kill you."

"Dirk's not my best friend. He's practically a stranger."

"He's your boyfriend."

Some boyfriend, I thought. "Sybil, we need to look for Baron and Milton. I'm not going to leave you until we find a way to stop the change."

"And if we don't?"

"We will," I replied. "Now, let's get out of here."

We took the long walk back up to the first floor. I had no idea where to look for the boys. For all I knew it was too late. They could already be zombies.

When we arrived back in the main corridor we heard

voices coming from down the hall. We exchanged a quick glance and headed in the direction of the voices.

I prayed it was Baron and Milton. Only they could end this nightmare and save my friend's life. As we got closer, we realized the voices were coming from Mrs. Mars' office.

A questioning look passed between us as we approached the office. The office door contained a huge pane of thick, opaque glass taking up most of the top half—impossible to see through.

Mrs. Mars was inside. She was arguing with someone.

"You failed!" she boomed in angry hoarse tones.

"Who's she talking to?" I whispered.

We crept up to the door, making sure we stooped below the glass pane so as not to be seen. We pressed our ears firmly against the wooden door. The sound of things crashing to the floor reverberated in the corridor as Mrs. Mars paced back and forth in silence.

"Is she arguing with herself?" I asked.

"Shh."

Suddenly she stopped, and I was certain she'd heard us. I held my breath, fully expecting the door to come flying open.

"Perhaps there's a way," she said. Her voice was much calmer now. Then she said something we couldn't make out, but the last part was crystal clear: ". . . and after that, Margot Jean Johnson, you are mine. Zombies rule!" she finished with a sinister, throaty chuckle.

Sybil and I looked at each other, astonished.

Mrs. Mars was the person who wanted us . . . *er*, me . . . dead . . . *er*, undead.

I took Sybil home with me. I bathed her wound in Betadine, then bandaged it in gauze. I fed her herbal tea—a chamomile, goldenseal, Red Zinger cocktail. I didn't know what else to do. But it seemed as though the change had slowed. Maybe I had caught it in time. Maybe she wasn't doomed. Maybe I wasn't fooling myself. Maybe.

As evening approached, with it came the fog of doubt.

Everything indicated Mrs. Mars was trying to turn us into zombies. I kept asking myself why. It didn't make sense. But I didn't need to know her reasons. If Mrs. Mars was the culprit, she held the key to the whereabouts of the antidote that could keep my friend from joining the living dead. I needed that key.

"We have to tell Principal Taft that Mrs. Mars got to Baron and Milton. And now she's trying to get us," Sybil said. She was lying on my bed, resting. The circles beneath her eyes had faded. They weren't as red as before.

"We need proof," I said.

"What kind of proof?"

"I don't know. Something she can't deny."

We sat in silence, and I thought about how many times we'd sat here in my room, eating snickerdoodles and planning our fabulous futures. Not once had our plans included surviving a zombie attack.

"We're telling the truth, right?" I said all of a sudden.

"Of course." She sat up, staring at me with the kind of schoolgirl anticipation she'd had when I'd told her some of my best-kept secrets.

I took a deep breath. "Remember Percy Paulson?"

"Your first kiss," she replied in a playful singsong.

"He wasn't. We didn't kiss that day after the walkathon." A look of surprise came across her face.

"What happened?"

"You left us alone to exchange phone numbers."

"I remember what *I* did, Margot."

"Right. Well . . . we didn't kiss."

"I thought he liked you?"

"He did . . . until I threw up."

Sybil shifted to the edge of the bed and stared at me. "*What?*"

"He leaned in to kiss me, and my stomach got all fluttery. And—blah!"

"How horrible!" She practically gasped.

"I didn't do it on him. No, no. Just a tiny bit on the ground. But I guess it was enough to make him not like me so much after that."

Sybil started to laugh, her laughter building like a musical crescendo, and then suddenly stopped.

"I wish you'd told me."

"I wanted to. But if I'd told you, I would have had to tell you why my stomach got all fluttery." I swallowed hard. "I was scared of being kissed."

She didn't laugh, or gasp, or look at me like I was from another planet. She eyed me thoughtfully.

"And all this time I thought he just didn't call."

"He didn't. . . . Well, maybe he did. I gave him a fake phone number." Sybil's eyes narrowed. "I was too embarrassed!"

"Why are you telling me this now?" she suddenly said. "You think I'm going to die, don't you?"

"No."

A beatific smile spread across her face. "Margot, I've never told you this before, but you're a lousy liar."

I laughed. It was the most genuine laugh I'd had in a long time.

"We're still telling the truth, right?" Sybil asked.

"Why stop now?"

She took a deep breath. "I only pretended to like Baron Chomsky to make you jealous."

"I know. It was pretty obvious. But you got him anyway. You got him without even trying," I said with a sigh.

"Sometimes you are so dumb. Baron isn't interested in me. He was doing the same thing I was doing, trying to get your attention."

Should I tell her how well it worked?

"That's why I didn't know about the antidote," she continued. "I wasn't hanging with Baron and Milton every night. I was only pretending to."

I was speechless, adjusting to the thought that perhaps Baron still liked me. For an instant my heart fluttered.

"I know you like him," Sybil said after a while. "You just don't want to date a geek. I can understand that. It's not in the manifesto."

I was red with embarrassment over all the bad things I had

thought about Baron and Sybil. Then suddenly I asked, "Do you think I'm fat?"

"Do you think I'm skinny?"

"No fair. You're answering a question with a question."

"I know, but since I'm the one who got bit, my rules."

"Okay." Then, "Yes."

She yelped. "I knew it!"

"But in a good way. If I had your legs I could wear thigh-high leather boots."

"If I had your chest I could wear revealing tops. And what a pleasure it would be to have hips to hold my pants up."

All of a sudden we were best friends again, trading body parts like we'd done back in middle school.

And now a brief note about body image: Isn't it amazing how we can't see the best in our own bodies? We are so envious of our friends and enemies. Imagine if we could learn to love ourselves just the way we are. It would put an end to zombie infestations around the world. . . . Okay, maybe it wouldn't do that, but it would be a good thing.

"Margot, I'm scared."

I guess it really was time to tell the truth.

"I'm scared, too."

"We've got to go back up to the school."

"I know."

A murky silence shrouded the room. Not long ago I would have been thinking about Dirk, or cheerleading uniforms, or the winter queen's first dance. I was overcome by shame for ever having those thoughts.

Sybil shifted to the end of the bed. "We need to go through Mrs. Mars' things. If she has the antidote we may find it tonight. If we wait, she may destroy it."

"She may have destroyed it already."

"But maybe she left a clue. If she did we'll find it tonight. Tomorrow may be too late . . . for me as well."

I nodded, standing up. "I should go alone. You're in no shape—"

"Margot, we're in this together," she said, stopping me mid-sentence. She got up off the bed.

I smiled. "I just can't get rid of you."

"Don't even try." We shared the best smile.

Going up to the school meant we had one hurdle to cross before we could carry out our plan—my parents. It was almost nine o'clock. They'd never let me go traipsing up to school at this hour.

"We'll tell them the truth," Sybil said.

"What? That all the kids at our school are zombies except us, and that while I was hanging decorations for the Winter Dance Mrs. Mars led a zombie attack against us? Oh, and speaking of zombies, that ravenous stud sitting next to you on the sofa with his hand in the chicken bucket is a zombie, too. Do I have it right?"

Sybil looked at me and sighed. "They'd send us off to the funny farm, wouldn't they?"

"Only if we were lucky." It was clear what we had to do.

We stopped off in the kitchen and retrieved the rotting fish I'd stuck in the back of the fridge. For weeks my parents had been asking about the smell. "Yeah, I smell it," I told them. "And I think it's high time you guys had a talk with Theo about the proper use of soap and water." Believe it or not, they had made him take a bath. Chalk one up for the good guys.

We rubbed the stinking fish all over our hands and faces, refilled our vials with fresh fish oil, and snuck out the back door.

And now a brief note about sneaking out: I want to state right here I'm not the kind of girl who sneaks out of the house after dark for late-night rendezvous with her friends. That's potentially dangerous. And so I want to go on record that I do not endorse girls sneaking out—unless they've been attacked by flesh-eating zombies, and need proof that their gym teacher is behind it. If that's the case, I think it's perfectly all right for you to slip by your parents and zombie boyfriend while they watch *Belly Dance Fitness Fusion* or some other ridiculous program and head out into the night. Okay?

Chapter
Twenty-nine

I'd been up to the school at night before, but only on special occasions: parent-teachers' night, the freshman dance. On those occasions, light spilling from the classroom windows seemed to fill the night air with a warm, inviting cheer. Tonight there was no light spilling from the windows. No warmth. No cheer. The only available light came from the streetlamps casting long, ominous shadows across the school's entrance. Inside, the building was bathed in darkness.

As we moved up the walkway, the large stone knights standing sentry seemed to be warning us to go home. We ignored their warning and walked right up to the door. That's when we realized the flaw in our plan. The door was locked and we didn't have a key.

"What now?" said Sybil. She was holding a Thermos of the herbal tea.

"I don't know. A window?"

The ground-floor windows were at least six feet off the ground. There was no way Sybil or I could reach any of them.

As I looked around for something to climb onto to boost myself up to the window ledge, Sybil stayed put. She needed her energy.

"Margot!" she suddenly called. Then she dove into the shrubbery by the front steps.

The front door was swinging open.

"Hide!"

But I didn't have time to run and hide. I was a few feet from the door; in a moment I'd be exposed.

Someone stepped out. Principal Taft. He set the cardboard box he was carrying on the ground.

I gasped.

His head swiveled toward me. Quickly, I stepped back into the shadows, pressed my body against the building, and held my breath. Taft looked right at me.

Just then a rustling in the bushes by the steps yanked his attention away. Taft's head spun around.

"Who's there?"

"*Meow.*"

Smiling with relief, he peered into the bushes. "Shoo," he said.

"*Meow.*"

"Go on! Git outta here!" He stomped his foot, and I heard a sound as if an animal had scampered away.

Satisfied the cat was gone, Principal Taft took a quick glance around, his eyes passing right by me. *He didn't see me.* He ducked back into the building.

Then, without thinking, just as the door was about to bang shut, I reached out and grabbed it.

I held the door open.

"Come on," I called.

Sybil scrambled out of the bushes. Her hair was a disaster.

There were tiny scratches on her arms and face, caused by the thorny brush. She was beginning to look like a zombie.

"You're a mess."

"Shouldn't you be thanking me for saving you from getting caught?"

"Oh. Yeah. Right. Thanks."

We held our breaths and entered.

I eased the door shut, thrusting us into near darkness. The soft light from the exit signs cast an eerie pall over the empty corridors. Principal Taft's footsteps moving away toward his office echoed in the darkness.

"Let's hide in the stairwell until he leaves," I said softly. "Then we can get on with our search."

The stairwell was darker than the corridor. We had crouched there for about five minutes when Sybil spoke.

"When I first moved here I was so worried about making friends."

"Lucky you. You caught me on the rebound."

Soft laughter rang out in the darkness.

"Remember how we first met?" she asked.

"How can I forget. You'd wrapped your arms around an old tree that was supposed to be bulldozed for the new shopping center. You gathered quite a crowd."

"You were the only girl in the crowd who joined me."

"Yeah," I said darkly. "Amanda and my ex-friends were laughing at you. I wanted to show them up."

"I'm glad you did."

More silence.

"You've changed," she said quietly. "Ever since you've become the it-girl and got a boyfriend, you're different. We used to have fun together."

"Yeah. We did." I would have said more, but I didn't want her to hear my voice trembling.

I *had* changed over the past seven weeks. I'd gone from insecure, to prideful, to . . . I don't know, something horrible. But now that the darkness within had been brought into the light, I recognized it wasn't a powerful force within me. It was nothing but fear, and jealousy, and pride—the fear of not being cool, or fashionable, or popular, or not having a boyfriend; the fear of being laughed at by Amanda Culpepper. I was jealous of my best friend, and too full of pride to admit it. Useless emotions.

"You really did do a good job as lunchroom monitor," I said. It was an apology of sorts.

"Thanks."

"I see why you chose it now. It seemed silly at first, but now I get it. You wanted to change the school's social structure, didn't you?"

She snorted out a laugh. "Yeah," she said. "What a silly idea."

"Why are you always trying to fix the world?"

"I don't know. Somebody has to. Why not us?"

I couldn't argue with that. I'd been chasing the status quo, and look where it had landed me.

Taft's approaching footsteps ended the discussion. He came into view carrying another cardboard box, which he set down as he eased open the door. The box clanked of empty cans. Then he picked up the box and exited the building, the door banging shut behind him. He was gone.

"What do you think Taft is doing here at night?" Sybil asked.

"He's the principal. Principals can't get enough of school. That's why they take the job in the first place."

"I suppose. But what if he and Mrs. Mars are in it together?"

Food for thought.

We made our way through the darkness to Mrs. Mars' office. We entered and turned on the light. While I had never been in the office before, it was clear someone had thrown a tantrum there. Many of her trophies and memorabilia were on the floor, some of them broken.

"She must have been pretty upset that the zombies didn't get us," Sybil said. Her voice was weak and scratchy.

I turned to her. Under the fluorescent lights I could see she had taken a turn for the worse. Her pale skin had acquired a green tint. The whites of her eyes were red again—her pupils dark stones set in deep sockets.

"Why don't you rest, Syb? I got this."

"I am a little tired."

She sat on the loveseat across from the desk, opened the Thermos, and sipped the tea. I began my search.

The walls of the office were adorned with framed photographs. Mrs. Mars was in each one, smiling and shaking hands with different women. In each photo there was a look of pride in her eyes. She wasn't scowling or leering. This was a side of Mrs. Mars I'd never seen. I thought I recognized one of the women, but I didn't know from where.

Eventually my search led to the closet. When I opened the door, a fragrance wafted out.

"Eww! What is that?" called Sybil.

My mind made an instant connection.

"I remember that smell," I said. "Stinky tennis shoes covered with cheese and then left out in the rain. . . . The vacant lot." My voice rose as the pieces fell into place.

"Yes! And in the corridor earlier, when someone was listening."

I dove into the closet. Two long, pleated skirts hung on old wooden hangers. A pair of black high-top industrial-strength gym shoes were in the corner—her daily uniform. I was beginning to go through her things when I remembered something else.

A low whistle escaped my lips. "Oh, man."

"What?"

"That swatch of fabric I found clinging to the nail. I just remembered where I'd seen it before. Mrs. Mars' scarf."

Mrs. Mars wore the same exact hideous blue scarf around her neck every single day. I was certain the fabric I had found clinging to the nail earlier was from her scarf.

I dug deeper into the closet. There was a simple cotton top on a hanger behind the pleated skirts. Neatly tied around the neck of the top was a torn blue silk scarf. I didn't have to put it up to my nose. The stench from the vacant lot was all over it.

I looked over at Sybil, my shoulders slumping. "She was so good at hounding me about the state endurance exam I didn't realize she was the zombie master. No wonder they were afraid of her."

"Did you find the antidote?"

I shook my head, and watched as the last vestiges of hope drained from her eyes. With each passing moment she was becoming more zombie-like. Her skin was paler, greener, crumblier.

"But I have a feeling the answer's right under our noses." Another lie. But I couldn't allow her to lose faith. I moved to the desk and began riffling through papers. Atop a neat pile was a letter addressed to my mother. A chill shot through me. I picked it up, holding it as if it were a time bomb that might go off at any moment.

"What is it?"

"A letter from Mrs. Mars to my mother." My hands were shaking.

"Read it."

Dear Mrs. Johnson,
Thank you so much for staying in such close touch with me
throughout the semester. How I do enjoy hearing from you.
I am writing today to clear up a little misunderstanding.
Some students believe the state endurance exam is about
running, jumping, and climbing. And while those things
are what a girl must do to pass, the exam itself represents
something more important. It represents character. I have
given up the notion of turning the modern teenage girl into
an athlete. But I haven't given up trying to build character
in these girls, and I believe enduring the rigors of the exam
does just that. Please pass this information on to your
amazing daughter. I look forward to having her in my class
again next semester, where we will have another go at the
state endurance exam—same bat time, same bat channel.

Very truly yours,
Eleanor Mars

Sybil was staring at me, waiting for me to say something.

"I don't get it," I said, rereading the letter. "Just something about me being in her class next semester and taking the state endurance exam. I thought she was going to pass me. She's crazy."

"Did she mention Baron or Milton, or the antidote?" Sybil asked. Her voice had gone raspy like sandpaper.

"No."

A bit more of the light of life disappeared from her eyes. She stood up. "Something's . . . happening to me."

"Hang on, Syb. We'll search the entire school if we have to."

She took a halting step toward me and went spilling to the floor. "Reeeahh." She mumbled something I couldn't make out.

I moved to her side, stooped, and cradled her in my arms. "You're going to be all right, Syb," I said soothingly, as tears sprang into my eyes.

She looked up at me. Her dark eyes were filled with ravenous desire. Her parched lips parted, and she rasped a single word. "Run!"

 "Sybil, I'm not leaving you."

"Isssokay." Her words slurred together. "I know you wouldn't llleave me. Butisss cool, really. You'll rrrrescue me later, after you find the annnidote."

"No! I'm not leaving you *until* we find the antidote. I'm not letting you become a zombie." I was trembling as I said the words. "Now, drink some tea."

"Yes, Mmmommy," she replied. The corners of her lips turned up slightly. A smile of sorts, that drained the tension from me.

"Maybe you were right about Taft. We'll search his office next," I said.

I willed away the tears and helped her to her feet. I scooped up the Thermos and her purse, and together we exited the office. When we stepped into the corridor, I sensed movement down at the far end. Squinting into the darkness, I could see something was coming toward us.

"Amanda," Sybil wheezed.

Amanda Culpepper and her gang of ghouls were moving through the shadows, coming at us.

"Ignore them," I said, recalling the last time I'd run into Amanda and her bunch. I knew they'd never bite me. I started walking toward the zombies.

"What are you doing?" Sybil cried, her tiny voice fearful.

"I'm going to Taft's office."

"But . . . what about them?"

"They won't bother us," I replied. My lips were tight. Sybil grabbed my shoulder and tried to pull me back. "Stop it!" I called, pushing her hand away. Realizing what I'd done, I turned to her, my voice softening. "Sybil, we may not have much time."

"But . . ." She pointed. Amanda was closing in on us. "What's she doing here, anyway?" she said in astonishment.

"Who cares?"

Amanda and the Zombiettes were now just twenty feet away.

"They're going to bite you," Sybil said.

Amanda's eyes were dead black stones fixed on me. The Zombiettes moaned as their lips parted, revealing teeth dripping saliva.

It's true, I thought. *They do want to bite me.*

All of a sudden, the pieces fell into place. Amanda's presence made perfect sense. *Of course they want to bite me now. They see themselves in me.* I had become as repulsive as they had been when they were alive. I was now the kind of girl I had promised myself I would never be. Like them, I had become a monster. The thought of it made me sick to my stomach.

I knew what I had to do. I stepped forward.

"They're going to bite you," Sybil repeated, fear coloring her words.

"I guess they are." Hungry eyes zeroed in on me as the Zombiettes closed. "Let them," I said.

Isn't this what I'd been wanting all semester? Amanda's bite would welcome me at long last into the sorority of popular girls forever. I'd roam the halls with Amanda and her girl ghouls—an it-girl for all eternity. I deserved no better. I'd shunned my best friend, betrayed Baron and Milton—the three people who had been trying to make things right.

I took another step forward. "Get out of here, Sybil."

"Margot, don't. I'm almost a zombie anyway. Save yourself," Sybil called, dramatically flinging herself at Amanda and the Zombiettes.

"Get out of the way, Syb. I *want* them to bite me." I jumped in front of her.

"What good would that do?" she said, her voice cracking.

"I deserve it. Now, run!"

"No, I deserve it. I should never have been jealous of you and Dirk." Sybil grabbed my arm and yanked me back.

I couldn't let the zombies bite my best friend. I had to do the right thing for once in my life. I shoved her out of the way, and she went spilling to the floor.

I faced Amanda. "Come on," I said. "Do it."

I thought about how life would be as a zombie, not caring about what I wore, or how fat I was, or what others thought of me. Not wondering if I should eat that extra snickerdoodle, or if a boy was ever going to ask me on a date. I knew I'd be giving up my individuality. But hadn't I given it up already by trying to be so much like Amanda?

"Wait a minute," Sybil said, getting up. "Margot, the girl in front of you is not a zombie."

"Grrrowl," Amanda snarled.

"Good. Great. Then you won't mind if she bites me."

"Zombies don't change their clothes." Sybil's accusing eyes moved to Amanda. "All semester long Amanda's been wearing a yellow sundress. Every single day the same yellow sundress. Tonight she's wearing a ball gown."

Sybil was right. I hadn't seen Amanda in the dress before.

"So?" I said dismissively. "Somebody changed her clothes. Maybe Mrs. Mars did it."

"No." Sybil snatched up the Thermos of tea and again jumped in front of me. "Amanda Culpepper, if you don't stop this charade I'm going to throw this Red Zinger and ruin your new dress."

"Grwl." Amanda continued toward us, but her growl had lost some of its sting.

Sybil unscrewed the cap and spilled a little of the red liquid out onto the floor for all to see. "That's silk," she called, brandishing the Thermos. "You'll never get the stain out."

"Grr," Amanda growled weakly.

Sybil hauled back, ready to throw. . . . That was when, for the first time in seven weeks, Amanda Culpepper spoke:

"Don't . . . you . . . dare!"

Just then, all the lights in the building came on.

Chapter
Thirty-one

 "You're . . . not a zombie!" I stammered in disbelief.

"Wow. And it only took you seven weeks to figure it out. I can see who got the genius genes in your family."

Amanda stood before us in a cream-colored Chanel ball gown, a self-righteous smirk playing on her lips. From up close it was obvious that her deep green pallor had been achieved with Halloween makeup, and her eyes were made dark by contact lenses. Amanda Culpepper was not a zombie. She was very much alive.

"Why?" Sybil asked. "Why would you pretend to be a zombie?"

"Why not?" Amanda replied matter-of-factly. "I mean, look at them." She gestured over her shoulder at the three undead heads behind her. "The poor things need direction. And I'm the only one who can give it to them."

I looked at the three zombies standing behind Amanda. They growled and snarled at us, but did not advance. "Why don't they attack? It's obvious we're human."

Amanda leaned in and whispered, "Those three would do *anything* to be members of the in-crowd. And without me there is no in-crowd, is there? So, they do what I say, even as zombies."

The PA system crackled to life. "Do You Really Want to Hurt Me," by Culture Club, began to play. I recognized it as one of the eighties tunes I'd programmed into Taft's computer for the dance.

"Well, I guess we should be getting to the dance," Amanda suddenly said. "I'm looking forward to being crowned winter queen."

Astonishment flashed across my face.

"Don't look at me like that." Laughter danced in her eyes. "That honor goes to the most popular girl at school. And let's face it . . . that's me."

"The Winter Dance is on Friday," I said, still trying to make sense of what was happening.

"Didn't you get the text? Oh, of course you didn't. The dance was moved to tonight. I guess that information was on a need-to-know basis, and you didn't need to know." Amanda was no less smug and self-righteous than she had been seven weeks ago.

A chill prickled along my spine. "Who sent the text?"

"I guess someone with some real authority around here. Duh!"

She turned and walked away. The Zombiettes shuffled after her.

I turned to Sybil. She was no longer standing. She was now lying on the floor, curled up into a fetal ball. I moved to her, stooping by her side.

"Amanda Culpepper's not a zombie. Wow," she rasped, looking up at me. The eyes no longer belonged to Sybil. They were monstrous pits that I didn't recognize. Her breath was coming short and quick, as if she were having an asthma attack.

"Whoever sent that text to Amanda is the zombie master. It seems the answer to all our questions is in the gym," I said.

"I know. Go," she said. "I'll be okay." I wasn't so sure about that.

"Drink some tea." I held the Thermos to her lips, and she drank.

"This is embarrassing," she said, drawing back and forcing a smile. She gripped the Thermos and gently pulled it from my hand. "I got this," she called. "Just go. Get to the gym, and find the antidote."

I didn't want to leave her, not like this. . . . But I had to. I gazed down the hall toward the gym. "I'll be back," I whispered.

"That's Baron's line." She was trying hard to get me to smile. I did.

I left Sybil sipping the tea and headed for the gym. I had the sickly feeling the next time I saw my friend she would be among the living dead. I wanted to tell her how sorry I was for the things I'd said and done, not just over the past seven weeks, but over the years. We always take the ones we love for granted, never taking the time to tell them how much we appreciate them—until it's too late. . . . Or maybe that's just me. I told myself the best way to show Sybil how much I cared was to bring back the antidote.

With Boy George's voice piping through the PA system, I headed for the gym. Blue and white streamers hung from the ceiling. Signs proclaimed: VOTE FOR MARGOT JEAN JOHNSON FOR WINTER QUEEN. YOU'LL GO FAR-GO WITH MARGOT.

I recalled the excitement of the previous year, when students huddled around the bulletin boards debating the prom queen candidates. I remember secretly wishing my name was among them.

Be careful what you wish for.

I walked into the gym. Dancing light bouncing off the foil snowflakes and musical notes hanging from the ceiling gave the room a sense of foreboding charm. Cocktail tables and chairs were set up all around, as if someone was expecting a crowd. The tables encircled a dance floor in the center of the gym. Someone had gone to a lot of trouble. But who?

Amanda and her crew were over by the punch bowls. Two of the Zombiettes had changed into matching purple ball gowns, obviously chosen to highlight Amanda's cream-colored gown. The third girl was still wearing the same grungy outfit she'd worn since the night of the carnival.

As I moved across the floor, "Everybody Wants to Rule the World," by Tears for Fears, started to play. As the guitars kicked, the lyrics ominously welcomed us to our lives, and warned there was no turning back.

How fitting.

I picked up a program from a side table and approached Amanda. She was gawking into her compact, applying red lip gloss that seemed just the right shade for her ghastly green complexion.

"Amanda, who's behind all this?"

"What difference does it make, um, what's your name again?" she said without looking up.

"You know my name."

"Dodgeball girl?"

"Ha-ha."

"Oh. Right. Margot."

"Amanda, I believe something bad is about to happen here."

"Relax, will you? There's nothing you can do about it now. It's over. You lost."

My breath caught in my throat as it suddenly dawned on me that Amanda was involved in the conspiracy.

She eyed me with mild interest. "I like the way you've been handling yourself these past weeks. You've got spunk. I could see us teaming up next semester." She went back to looking in the tiny mirror. "We might be in a new school next semester. I can see us now, walking in together on the first day, dressed in killer outfits. Even the teachers will be jealous."

"I need the antidote, Amanda, and I need it now." My voice was low, yet filled with rage.

She looked at me as if she had no idea what I was talking about. "Sometimes, Margot, you sound like you come from another planet."

Okay . . . maybe I was wrong about Amanda. She was too stupid and self-centered to be a part of the conspiracy. I changed the subject. "How come that one's not in a formal?" I pointed at the zombie girl still wearing her grungy clothes.

"Oh, Heather? It's sad really." She snapped shut the compact and walked me out of earshot. "I gave her that hideous top for her birthday last year. It was a cheap rag I got off a sale rack at some *discount* house." She infused the word *discount* with distaste. "And because *I* gave it to her, it held special meaning." She glanced over at Heather to make sure she hadn't moved. She hadn't. Heather and the others stood where she'd left them, awaiting her next command. Amanda continued.

"If she only knew how many laughs we got from her wearing that ugly thing, she'd throw it right in the trash. Anyway, something in her bones is telling her the top is special—it's not."

"I thought you guys were friends."

She shot me an incredulous look. "We are. Best friends. But she has eyes; she can see. She's wearing that monstrosity because she wants to. That's what's so funny about it." She laughed out loud.

I looked back over at Heather and the others. They were still waiting for Amanda to show them some attention.

Suddenly the music stopped, and Principal Taft entered. He was wearing a tuxedo with the bow tie hanging open around his neck. Quite dapper.

"Oh, wow. Principal Taft is the zombie master."

"Shh . . . Quiet. This is where I get my crown."

Principal Taft was holding a mic in his hand. He moved to the center of the room.

"Ladies and uhh . . . ladies. Welcome to Salesian High School's Winter Dance. This auspicious event was the brain-child of one of Salesian's finest students, Junior Margot Jean Johnson." He clapped. No one joined him. There were only two of us available to clap. I didn't clap for myself, and Amanda stood there looking bored.

"Get to the good part," she called.

"Oh, yes. And now the moment I've been waiting for for quite some time." He looked at us. "Margot, Amanda, before I announce the crowning of the winter queen, your fellow classmates have prepared a special honor for the both of you."

At that precise moment, all the gymnasium doors flew open. Standing in the doorways for as far as the eye could see were our zombie classmates, all in prom attire.

"*Welcome to the zombie dance!*" Taft bellowed. Zombies began filing in, hundreds of them, filling up the gym, heading in our direction.

 "What about my tiara?" Amanda called to a fleeing Taft.

Taft ran across the gym and let himself out through a side door. Of course, that option was no longer available to us. Our only escape route was through the sea of zombies.

"This sucks!" Amanda groused after he was gone.

"Yeah," I agreed. "Big-time."

Zombies continued filing in.

The music started up again: "She Blinded Me with Science," by Thomas Dolby.

Amanda rushed over to join Heather and the other girl ghouls. She started barking out orders. But the Zombiettes weren't paying her any attention. Heather bared her teeth and grabbed Amanda by the arm.

"Stop it!" Amanda shrieked. She tried to pull away, but Heather's grip was too strong.

"Hhhhhhh." Heather's lips parted.

Without thinking, I raced across the room and rapped her sharply on the nose with my rolled-up program.

"Yeeee!" She released Amanda, letting out a high-pitched whine.

"Sorry about that. . . . By the way, cute top," I called as I pulled Amanda away.

"Where are we going?" she squawked.

"I don't know."

The gym was quickly filling up with angry zombies. We had three, four minutes tops before we'd be attacked. I began looking around for another escape route, or a weapon, anything that could prolong our ordeal.

That's when I noticed the ropes.

I yanked Amanda over to the wall and pulled on the cord releasing the ropes from the ceiling. Four thick, braided ropes dropped down.

Amanda eyed the ropes, her nose in the air. "What?"

"It's our only way out, Amanda. We'll climb them, and stay up until Sybil can rescue us."

"Sybil isn't going to rescue us."

She was probably right about that.

"She might. We have to try."

"This is a thousand-dollar Chanel ball gown!" Amanda whined. "It has no business on the ropes."

Somehow, I had to get Amanda to climb the rope. "Look," I said, pointing at the swarm of zombies nearing us. "Goths. You're about to become a Goth for all eternity."

She eyed the Goths with disdain. "Ugh! That monochromatic color scheme. How boring."

"I know."

"And I believe they apply their makeup with a trowel."

"I know."

"And talk about bad hair days. I've never seen one with a good hair day."

"I know!" I exclaimed as the Goths got closer. "And you'll have to listen to Goth pop . . . Evanescence."

She brightened a bit. "I could handle Evanescence. That Amy Lee's got—"

"Okay, forget about the Goth pop. Just keep thinking black. Nothing but black. Everyday black. All black, all the time . . . Black."

"Oh, my goodness!" Amanda shrieked, shooting the nearing Goths one last withering glance.

She began to climb.

I scrambled up the adjacent rope as the zombies closed in. The thick hemp ripped into my hands and knees. My palms burned with the pain of a thousand paper cuts, yet this time I continued upward.

Just then the song changed. "You Keep Me Hangin' On" filled the air.

Amanda struggled up the rope in the voluminous ball gown. The zombies below swatted at her heels. One snatched at her shoe, and she kicked it off as she shimmied up and out of reach. "My arms are killing me!" she called.

My arms hurt as well. I was grateful for the little practice Mrs. Mars had insisted I get in gym class. But I still wasn't in any kind of shape, and my feeble muscles screamed in protest.

"Hang in there," I called back. I looked down at the horde of zombies gathering below and was surprised to see they were no longer divided into cliques. Prep zombies stood shoulder-to-shoulder with nerds, stoner nerds with emos—all working together to get at us.

At that moment thoughts of Sybil flared through my mind. She'd called her desire to change the school's social structure a silly idea. But it wasn't. She had actually gotten various groups to roam with one another. It's not like they were hanging out or anything—they were zombies. But she got them to coexist peacefully, not snarking at one another, or gossiping behind one another's backs, or getting jealous when one of their friends liked a cute boy. The zombies had just one thing in common— they were zombies. But we kids have a whole lot in common. Shouldn't it be easier for us to hang together?

A wave of shame flooded through me. While I had been busy living out the lie of being the most popular girl at school, Sybil had realized that being popular wasn't the be-all and end-all of high school existence. To her, we were all the same.

Some of the zombies started jumping to get at us. They pushed and shoved one another to be first in line to dig their teeth into us. This sent the ropes swinging back and forth. The swinging motion made it harder to hang on. They were inadvertently shaking the ropes the way one might shake a tree to make an apple fall.

"Stop that!" Amanda yelled down at the zombies. She looked at me. "I can't hold on much longer." She looked down again. "Look, there's Kim Travers. She's a mathlete. Maybe she'll bite me. I've always wanted to be good at math." I could tell from the look on her face she was giving in to the idea of becoming a zombie. Her grip loosened.

"I don't think it works like that, Amanda," I said quickly. "All you'll be is a math geek zombie."

"Oh?" she said as she considered this. Her grip on the rope tightened.

The gym had fifteen-foot windows that looked out onto the campus. Through them I could see the walkways that wound through campus, lined with light posts that gave off soft yellow light. The world outside was quiet, green, safe. It seemed warm and inviting.

Since middle school I'd been an outsider wanting in. Now,

as I hung high above the gym floor teeming with zombies, I wanted out.

"Hey, Amanda, remember Baron Chomsky and Milton Sharp?"

"Who?"

"Two geek boys, one imitates James Bond all the time and the other wears T-shirts with goofy cartoon characters on them."

"Hello? I have other things on my mind right now." She gestured toward the moaning horde below.

"I know, but it looks like we're going to be up here for a while. Do you know who I'm talking about?"

She thought about it for like a nanosecond. "Yes, I know who you mean." She was clearly annoyed with the conversation.

"I was just wondering if you'd seen them around?"

"I can't remember. I don't keep tabs on geeks."

"Of course you don't. But I mean, since everyone else is a zombie, they would have been easy to spot."

The floor below had become a virtual sea of zombies, all aching to get at us.

She sighed. "If you must know, I've seen them quite a bit. They were always giving the jock zombies wedgies, or hanging KICK ME signs on their backs, or placing morsels of food on their heads. So childish."

"Yeah," I said, smiling as I pictured Baron toying with the zombies. I recalled the look of pride on his face the day he'd shown me and Sybil the wedgie he'd given the jock zombie. "Did you know they disappeared a few days ago?"

"I couldn't care less. I'm going to disappear in a few minutes if you don't figure out a way to get us out of here."

I ignored her snarky tone. "Did you know they invented an antidote that could change everyone back?"

Her eyes widened, and I could tell she was hearing this for the first time. "What? And they didn't use it? Idiots! I guess they thought they'd be better off keeping everything as it is so they could be big shots."

No, that was me.

"If I'd had a cure, I would have changed things back a long time ago. You have no idea how hard it is being popular when there's no one to flaunt it in front of."

Actually, I did know.

"That's probably why Principal Taft locked them in the boiler room."

My body stiffened as my eyes widened.

"At the time I thought it was some kind of detention for teasing the zombies. But he probably wanted them and their antidote out of the way."

It was good knowing what had happened to my friends. I wondered if they were still among the living. Before I could deal with that, however, there was something I needed to get off my chest.

"You know, Amanda, for as far back as I can remember I've wanted to be you."

"Well, of course you do. Who wants to be a nobody?"

"Back when I thought you were a zombie, I would have let you bite me, so that I might roam the halls of Salesian by your side for all eternity. Before you became a zombie, I wanted to hang with you. If you'd said, 'Margot, you look cute today,' I would have rejoiced, and if you'd said, 'I hate those shoes' I would have taken them home and burned them."

Note to self: You really have to start writing some of this stuff down—it's brilliant!

I continued: "What a fool I've been wasting my time on you."

The smug smile that graced her lips slowly faded. She hung there above the zombies, staring at me. Her eyes narrowed.

"I've never liked you."

"You just asked me to hang out with you next semester."

"I don't need to like you to hang with you," she said.

"Is that why you stopped talking to me after seventh-grade summer camp?" The question flew from my lips so quickly I didn't realize I was going to ask it. It was a question I'd been torturing myself about since I was twelve years old. I knew the answer would never free me from the years of pain the snub had caused. Still, I had to know. As I stared at her, waiting for her reply, a lump formed in my throat.

"Oh, that," she said. "I guess I did like you until that summer."

"What did I do to make you guys stop talking to me?"

"Okay. You know how every night when we went to our bunks we always gossiped about someone? Remember how much we looked forward to lying in bed in the darkness, gossiping?"

I nodded.

"Well, after you went home sick, we gossiped about you. We made a bunch of stuff up—like we always did—but this time, it was about you."

"What kind of stuff?"

"The usual. You smelled bad; you talked about us behind our backs; you didn't know how to dress. You know?"

I was getting a sinking feeling, because I *did* know. We'd said those same things about other girls all the time. Not so much fun when it was about me.

"And since you weren't there to defend yourself, we all decided we hated you."

"But that's not fair," I said. It was the voice of a twelve-year-old girl. I could feel myself getting sick to my stomach, like

I had when they first stopped talking to me. "It wasn't true. You guys just made up a bunch of lies."

She shrugged. "You asked, I told," she said in a dismissive tone.

"We used to do everything together. I thought we were friends."

"We *were* friends," she replied. If there was a hint of remorse in her words, I didn't hear it.

"All these years I thought I'd done something wrong. I tried so hard to get you to like me again." My words were filled with years of anguish.

"Really?" She seemed surprised.

"Yeah!" It was embarrassing admitting it.

"Let me give you some advice. The next time you want someone to like you, try sucking up to them a little more."

Hadn't thought of that. I guess I just wanted her to like me for me. What a concept—liking someone for who they are.

"You're the worst kind of person, you know that?" I suddenly said.

She thought about this for a second. "Of course *you'd* say that. You're a nobody. I'd rather be me than you any day."

I knew she'd say something like that. Sadly, there was a time when I'd rather have been her than me, too. I'd been blinded by all of Amanda's surface glitter.

I realized as I hung there that getting the chicken pox that seventh-grade summer was actually a blessing in disguise, because it allowed me to meet Sybil. Sybil would never tell lies about me behind my back, or desert me. She was an amazing person, a great friend. I hadn't been taking care of that friendship—until now.

I looked Amanda in the eye. "I know you think you're better than me. That's what makes girls like you so sad. Your reality is clouded by some distorted image of yourself. People like me help you keep that image alive by wanting to hang with you, fawning over you all the time. But I'm not doing that anymore." I took a deep, cleansing breath and let it out slowly. It felt soo good. "By the way, I'm not a nobody. I'm somebody. The name's Johnson, Margot *Jean* Johnson."

And with that, I released my grip on the rope and dropped, plummeting into the outstretched arms of the zombies below.

Chapter

Thirty-three

I landed—*thoomph!*—on my back, atop the zombies' raised hands. So far so good. Now came the hard part. Like a partygoer at a club, stage diving into the crowd, I had to allow the zombies to crowd-surf me across the room toward the door.

I'd seen crowd-surfing on TV and in movies, and had always wanted to try it. How exciting it had to be to be carried away on an ocean of partying people. Of course, my parents had warned me against it: *Too dangerous. You'll break your neck. Promise us you'll never do that.* But as I'd weighed the options available to me hanging above the gym floor, I figured it was worth the risk.

The key to zombie-surfing was not to fight, but to give in and allow myself to be moved freely. The zombies began working me away from the ropes across the room. I looked up into the horrified face of Amanda. She thought I'd given up. I *had* given up . . . on her. Then her expression slowly changed as she realized I'd planned the entire maneuver. I was escaping.

Suddenly, Amanda came plunging down. *CARUNCH!* The zombies parted, allowing her to go crashing to the floor. As she struggled to her feet, she was surrounded. They'd hated her and the humiliation she'd inflicted upon them throughout their school lives. They saw their chance, and all wanted a piece of her.

She glanced around as the knot of zombies around her tightened. Heather was at the front of the pack.

"Hi, Heather," she said cautiously, donning a fake smile.

The zombies moved in.

"Um . . . That top looks so good on you. When this is over, I'm going to give you another one just like it for your birthday."

And they were on her.

"*Aiiiiiieeeee!*"

Her shrieks filled the air, along with moans of zombie glee, and swatches of Chanel ball gown. The zombies holding me up dropped me. They too wanted a piece of her. For now, I was forgotten.

I eased out of the gym and raced up the corridor, praying I wasn't too late to save Sybil. Her friendship was more precious to me than it had ever been. I decided to go and check on her before I went looking for the geeks, who hopefully had the antidote.

I returned to the spot in the corridor where I'd left her.

She was gone.

The Thermos lay on the floor in a puddle of red tea. All the air went out of me, and I sank to my knees. I could feel my desire to live slipping away. I thought back to all the nights we'd sat up in my bedroom planning our fabulous high school careers, all the days since the eighth grade when we'd been there for each other.

I don't know where it came from, but thoughts of the good times filled me with new resolve.

I got up.

"Taft!" I bellowed at the top of my lungs. My words echoed through the empty corridor. "Walk This Way," by Run DMC, played in the background.

Taft had pulled off this deception by playing on my desire to be popular. Sybil had wanted to go to the authorities right away, but I had convinced her going along with Principal Taft was best. *Idiot!*

I moved down the hall, energized by my new resolve. Suddenly Taft stepped from around the corner at the intersection in the corridor. He was smiling as I approached.

"Margot Jean Johnson." He shook his head with remorse. "What a fatal fiasco this is. A truly tragic turn of events. I really liked you."

"Then why?"

"You gave me no choice. You've changed, Margot. The girls I enlisted blended in with the pack. They did what was expected. But now look at you—the way you dress, the way you act, the way you think. The old Margot would never have figured out how to thwart the zombies. She would have been too busy trying to fit in with them. I'm afraid you've become an individual."

"Isn't that what school is supposed to teach us?"

He chuckled. "Of course not. A school runs on order. Sameness. That's why we have up and down staircases. That's why you raise your hand instead of calling out, everyone following the rules, everyone conforming. If all you kids decided to become individuals we'd have anarchy. And we can't have that."

"No offense, Principal Taft, but that's crazy."

His eyes widened. "I am not insane," he said softly.

"I didn't say—"

"Zombies are the best thing that's ever happened to this school. No discipline problems, perfect attendance, no fights in the cafeteria, no one threatening the teachers, everybody where they're supposed to be when they're supposed to be there . . . except you." His eyes narrowed. "The sooner you become a zombie, Margot, the sooner things can get back to the way they should be around here."

"So, it's true. You're the one who turned everyone into zombies?"

He nodded.

"What about Mrs. Mars?"

He snorted. "What about her? Don't give her any credit for this."

"But she must have been your accomplice."

He snorted again. "Why? Because kindly Principal Taft couldn't possibly have done this without help from tough-as-nails Mrs. Mars? Ha! It was all me."

"But I heard her. 'Zombies rule!' "

He smiled. It was a smile filled with beneficence. "This school has a fabulous intercom system. Not only can I talk to every classroom on campus, I can listen in as well. I recorded Mrs. Mars talking to you girls throughout the semester. Did you know that with a little help from Pro Tools editing software, I can manipulate her words to make it seem as if she's saying almost anything? It pays to be computer savvy." He winked at me.

"Anyway, after my unsuccessful attempt in the gym, I lured you girls to her office and played a tape for you."

"But the scarf . . . the odor."

He raised his hand. "Me again. The stink is an unfortunate side effect of the formula that contains the virus. I used it to my advantage, to throw you girls off the scent . . . so to speak."

I stared at him, shaking my head, as the reality of his clever trap washed over me. "Stinky tennis shoes covered with cheese and then left out in the rain," I said softly.

"Excuse me?"

"You have to have a kid brother to understand."

"I'm sure you see that somebody had to fix things before they got too far out of hand." When I didn't respond, he sighed and shook his head, as if I weren't bright enough to understand. "Principals across the nation are at their wits' end the way you modern kids act out. And your parents aren't doing anything to help. When I become district supervisor, I'm going to see to it that every student in the district is a zombie. This thing is going to get popular."

"You're wrong about one thing, Principal Taft," I said.

"What's that?"

"You *are* crazy."

"Well . . . you're entitled to an opinion. At least you are for now."

"How did you do it? I know it had something to do with the carnival."

He smiled. "Believe it or not, the whole thing started in an Internet chat room. Administrators around the country were grousing about the sad state of students these days. Then someone chimed in and said they had a solution. A virus, of sorts, that makes people conform."

"So, it *is* a virus?" It was good to know that Baron and Milton had diagnosed correctly.

"Yes. I didn't know what I was getting myself into when I

purchased it. But I needed to do something if I wanted that promotion." He looked at me, as if for confirmation, before going on.

"The instructions said it had to be ingested. And if more than fifty percent of the student population took it, they would see to it that the rest conformed. So I paid a vendor at the carnival to add it to all the soft drinks. It was that simple."

He chuckled, pleased with himself. "The person who sold me the virus didn't say anything about zombies. I was so nervous those first few days of the outbreak. I honestly couldn't have gotten this far without you, Margot. But now look. That virus is the best thing that's ever happened to this school."

I'd heard enough of his lunatic rantings. "I need the antidote," I demanded. "Where is it?"

"There is no antidote." There was a finality to his words that blanketed me in a wave of despair. Game, set, and match. "I think it's appropriate you and your friend become zombies at the same time. I tried that once before in the gym, but you outsmarted me."

"Where is she? If you've harmed her—"

"Of course I didn't harm her." He sounded almost hurt by the accusation. "What kind of principal do you think I am? Margot, I'm not a bad man. I'm a concerned administrator."

"Then where is she?"

"She's where you guys meet up all the time. Sitting in front of her locker waiting for you . . . *Duh!*"

I left Principal Taft and went in search of Sybil. I had to rescue Sybil and the geek boys before the zombies in the gym came looking for us. "I Want Candy" was playing as I headed up the corridor.

Just as Taft had said, she was seated in front of her locker.

What he had neglected to say is that she was tied to a student desk. She was coiled in thick rope. Her hands and feet were bound. Her head was down, listing to the side as if she'd been drugged.

"Sybil! It's me!" I called.

I started running. I was going to rescue her. Knowing this made me oblivious to the danger around me. I was doing something for somebody else. Pride surged through me.

She lifted her head as I got closer, and I realized it wasn't Sybil tied to the chair. It was Mrs. Mars.

When she saw me, an odd smile appeared on her lips. I gazed into her eyes. They were deep red, her skin green and flaky. A low rumbling commenced deep in her chest.

I reached her and began to untie the rope.

"Stop him!" Her voice was sandpaper over rough wood.

I realized there was something else in her eyes, a warning.

She was looking above her head. My eyes followed and I saw it. It was an old trick, one I'd seen in movies, heard stories of kids pulling since grade school. In its original form someone balances a bucket of water above a partially opened door. When the victim enters and pushes the door all the way open—*splash!* Loads of humiliating fun.

This version was slightly different. An old aluminum washtub was suspended from the light fixture above Mrs. Mars. I could see the nearly invisible fishing line that extended from the washtub to the chair. If the chair moved the washtub would dump its contents onto her.

Acid? I wondered. *Boiling oil?*

"I see it," I cried. There was a simple solution—free her without moving the chair. "Keep still," I said. "I can do this."

Her eyes widened.

"Don't worry. I'm rescuing you. The key is not moving the chair."

"Mmmmmaaaah!"

My fingers froze on the knots as I heard the familiar zombie moan coming from Mrs. Mars. . . . *SPLOOSH!*

The washtub spilled a saucy brown concoction all over me.

Suddenly Mrs. Mars' chest heaved. A moment later she was struggling wildly against the rope to free herself. She eyed me hungrily, growling, hissing, and snapping. I was too late. She had crossed over. If I freed her now she would attack.

I took a step back. "I'm sorry, Mrs. Mars," I whispered. "I'm too late." My words were filled with genuine remorse.

"Sorry I had to fool you like that." The voice of Principal Taft behind us. "In case you're wondering, that's canned beef chili. The chunky kind." His words were cheerful. The man was totally bonkers.

I faced him. "You know, in most books the villain makes one final appearance. I do believe this is your second," I said, my voice reeking with sarcasm.

"I'm not a villain," he said calmly. "In fact, I'm the good guy; I'm a concerned administrator."

"You turned Mrs. Mars into a zombie."

"I didn't want to. But at the last faculty meeting she threatened to expose me. She was the only opposition to my plan."

"All the other teachers were zombies."

He stroked his chin. "True. Mrs. Mars threatened to go to one of her big-shot former students. She said she'd given my way a chance, but she felt it lacked vision."

"I can't believe she became a zombie so quickly."

"She's old," he said. "She doesn't have Sybil's youthful immune system. I guess the older they are, the faster they change." He was smiling again.

For some reason at that moment the photos on Mrs. Mars' wall flashed through my mind. I suddenly understood that the mementos were photos of Mrs. Mars with former students, students she was proud of. The woman in the photo I had recognized was Senator Watson. Senator Watson had gone to Salesian.

"What does she know about vision?" Taft said, scowling at her. "She's a gym teacher." He looked at me as if he was waiting for me to tell him he was right.

Considering all the successful women who graced Mrs. Mars' walls, it seemed to me she had quite a bit more vision than he did.

"You're a horrible man," I said.

He smiled. "Some people don't understand progress. But if it makes you feel any better, I didn't do this to her. That honor goes to your friend, Sybil."

"No." The word was dead on my lips.

"Yes." He nodded somberly.

If Sybil had done this to Mrs. Mars, that meant she hadn't made it, either. My earlier despair was child's play compared to how I was feeling in that moment. I wanted to cry out *"Nooo!"* But I wouldn't give him the satisfaction. Besides, getting emotional wouldn't fix anything, and I had a lot of fixing to do.

Principal Taft couldn't have been more pleased with himself. "Now, I'm thinking Mrs. Mars is a zombie, Sybil is a zombie, and you're still here. What is wrong with this picture?"

"If it's the last thing I do, I am going to stop you."

He ignored the threat. "Remember when I told you zombies love meat, hate fish? Well, you are covered with tender chunks of sirloin. That's what the can said: 'beef chili made with tender chunks of sirloin.' I bet you're irresistible to zombies now."

A self-satisfied smile appeared on his lips. "I don't think you need to worry about a boyfriend anymore. I do believe you're about to have all the boyfriends you can handle."

In the distance, I could hear the sound of many footsteps moving in our direction. The footsteps weren't shuffling. Whoever was coming was running up the corridor. People, I thought. Living, breathing human beings were on their way.

As the footsteps got closer, echoing as they slapped against the tile floor, the triumphant expression on Taft's face slowly began to fade.

"You hear that?" I said, a hint of hope creeping into my voice. "Someone's coming to rescue me. Sybil must have called for help before she became a zombie."

Just then, six tall and athletic zombies came running around the corner, dressed in Salesian High track uniforms. They stopped when they saw us. There was yearning in their eyes.

Chapter
Thirty-four

I recognized the six zombies standing before us. They were all members of the school's track team. Among them was Tyler Moss. Tyler was long and lanky, a top-notch sprinter who'd won several gold medals for the 100-meter dash. He was at one time the most feared sprinter in the state. Now, he was a ferocious-looking zombie.

Taft was smiling again. "I love yanking your chain," he said with a chuckle. "You should have seen the look on your face when you thought you were being rescued."

"Fast zombies," I said. There was no emotion attached to the words. It was an observation.

"Yes," Taft replied. He was gloating. "These kids have been running all their lives. They're my überzombies. Margot, if it's any consolation, you really were my favorite."

"You can turn off the compliments, Principal Taft. I think when you're about to kill someone a compliment loses its charm."

He thought about this a moment. "I can see that. But you always wanted to feel special, right? Now you're about to get turned by überzombies. That'll put you right at the top of the zombie social order."

The zombies began to moan. Their ravenous eyes crawled over us.

"Let's Hear It for the Boy," by Deniece Williams, pumped through the sound system.

"You can thank me later," Principal Taft continued. "The boys are getting hungry. It may take several hours for you to become a zombie, but don't worry. You'll be joining your friend soon enough. Now, I've got to get home."

He began inching away from the zombies, who were now focused on me. Then he turned the corner and was gone. I could hear the *click-click* of his shoes as he hightailed it out of the building.

Slowly, the überzombies advanced.

"I'm getting so sick of zombies coming after me," I whispered.

The zombies had fanned out into a circle around me, and were closing in. There would be no escape. There was no way I could outrun them.

"So, Tyler Moss, you are looking very buff these days. Been working out?"

His only response was the desire in his eyes.

"Did I ever tell you I had a big ole crush on you freshman year?"

Tyler's lips parted. "Mmmmmm."

"See, that! I thought you had a thing for me. Look, why don't we all go back inside, do the electric slide, and talk about this tomorrow?"

"Mmmmaaah!" Mrs. Mars cried, as she struggled against the ropes. The ropes were loosening. In a moment I'd have her to worry about as well.

It was then I noticed that the zombies stopped advancing

when Mrs. Mars cried out. Quickly, I got behind her desk and shoved it forward a few inches. The zombies all backed off a few feet.

"Mrs. Mars, you're my ticket out of here."

I pushed her desk a few inches toward the zombies. They began backing down the hall.

"Mmmmaaah!" Mrs. Mars repeated as she continued to struggle.

"I know this isn't a moment we're going to look back on with pride, Mrs. Mars. But I want you to know I do possess the character you spoke of in the letter to my mother. You'll see."

I grabbed the top of her chair, tilted it backward, and began dragging her up the corridor away from the überzombies.

"Don't you boys move!" I called, imitating her gravelly voice as I'd done earlier in the gym. "Or you'll be in my class next semester, same bat time, same bat channel."

The überzombies were standing still, seemingly befuddled. Then my gaze moved ahead, up the corridor, in search of an escape route. The elevator was at the end of the corridor, but I needed a key to operate it.

"Do you have a key to the elevator on you, Mrs. Mars?"

Her answer was an angry growl.

I stopped dragging, moved back around in front of her, and began rifling through her pockets. I pulled out a large ring of about twenty keys.

"I sure hope one of these is what I'm looking for."

I resumed dragging her, now with purpose, toward the elevator at the end of the corridor. For their part, the überzombies were beginning to overcome their fear. Cautiously, they again began advancing on us.

We reached the elevator, and systematically I began trying keys in the lock.

"Grrrowl." Mrs. Mars' chest heaved upward, and the ropes around her went slack.

She was free.

It would be only moments before she realized it. I fumbled key after key into the lock.

Click. The key in my hand turned the tumblers. I pressed the call button. It lit up. In the distance I could hear the ancient elevator rumbling to life.

Mrs. Mars stood, the ropes pooling around her ankles. The überzombies again halted their advance.

"Good, Mrs. Mars. Just keep them at bay for a few more minutes."

The sound of the elevator stopping made my heart dance. Mrs. Mars turned to me.

"Hhhhhh." Her lips parted and she emitted a deep, airy sigh. Her gnarled fingers reached for me just as the elevator door opened. I scrambled into the elevator and mashed all the buttons. Nothing.

"Come on! Close door! Close!"

Mrs. Mars sluggishly began moving toward me. She slogged onto the elevator and again reached for me. I scurried into a corner. I thought about making a run for it, but the überzombies were now standing at the elevator threshold, not willing to go any farther. I'd be walking into their open arms.

Bing!

The door slid shut. *Clunk.* Then the tiny chamber began to move upward. Mrs. Mars stepped toward me. I knew if I eased backward, in seconds I'd be trapped in a corner. So I darted toward her, and as she reached for me I dashed behind her. Now her back was to me.

She turned around as quickly as she could. But she was a zombie, and an old zombie at that, so her movements were sluggish. As she turned to her right, I moved to my left, keeping her back in front of me.

"Mrs. Mars, you really don't want to bite me. I'm going to be your prize student next semester. We just need to get past this moment in time."

She flung her arms behind herself, trying to grab me while her back was to me. I dodged her grasp.

"Graaagh!" she screamed in frustration. She jerked to her left, and I jumped to my right. She jerked to her right, and I jumped to my left.

"We're going to laugh about this one day," I called.

Several dodgy minutes later, the elevator door finally opened, and I blasted out, away from the clutches of Mrs. Mars.

I was running . . . *fast*. Fear is an amazing drug. It allows you to do things you never thought possible. Tonight I had run, used my strength, and even climbed the ropes—everything I needed to do for the state endurance exam. That's why I knew I'd be ready next semester. What I didn't want to think was . . . *if there is a next semester.*

"I Ran," by A Flock of Seagulls, began to play. I headed up the corridor as fast as my aching legs would allow. I took the stairs back down to the main-floor corridor, then barreled toward the main exit door. If I was going to save Sybil I needed to get some help.

I slammed into the door with a booming thud—*CARUNCH!* I bounced off the heavy door like a rubber ball. Quickly I recovered and pressed on the metal bar to release the catch. The door crept open six inches, then stopped. *Clunk.* I put my back against the door, pushing with all my might. *Clunk, clunk, clunk.*

The door had been chained from the outside. Principal Taft was making sure I didn't get away this time.

The überzombies emerged from around the corner. I took off up the corridor.

Slap, slap, slap, slap . . .

The überzombies' footsteps reverberated in the empty corridor behind me. And while they may not have been as fast as when they were human, the track zombies moved with amazing speed.

I ran from corridor to corridor trying all the exits. Every door had been locked and chained from the outside. With every futile step the zombies got closer.

A searing pain in my lungs. My achy legs slowed. I couldn't go much farther.

I have to make it to the boiler room. Maybe Baron and Milton are still among the living. Maybe the three of us could stand a chance against the zombies.

It was a feeble plan, but a plan nonetheless, and it gave me hope. With the hope came the burst of energy I desperately needed.

My lungs were on fire as I took the stairs to the basement. The überzombies were close on my heels. There was only one staircase that led to the boiler room. It was clear across the building. A long way to run with überzombies on your tail. *I have to make it there*, I told myself.

The zombies were closing fast.

"Run!" I called, urging myself on. If only I had done those practice runs around the track as Mrs. Mars had suggested.

Too late to think about that now.

The cafeteria was to my left. Without thinking, I crashed through the double swinging doors into darkness.

It was empty, chairs neatly folded atop tables. . . . And dark, lots of shadows to hide in. I ducked behind a table. If I caught my breath, maybe I could make a run for it.

Two beams of fuzzy light shone through the windowpanes in the double doors. Phil Collins' "Against All Odds" played in the background.

There was a throbbing pain in my left ankle. I'd twisted it along the way. The ankle had a knot on it the size of an orange. Running would be even more difficult from here on in.

I needed to make a stand. How many zombies could I rap on the nose with a rolled-up newspaper before one grabbed me? That's something they never teach in math class.

Or maybe I could use the zombie death grip. I smiled as I thought of Baron teaching Sybil the grip the night we went to Dirk's house. I was so blinded by jealousy I couldn't see he was doing it to get my attention.

I like Baron.

There, I finally admitted it to myself. He wasn't the kind of boy I wanted to be associated with. He wasn't popular, or an athlete, or a member of any of the cliques Amanda and the it-girls would ever date. He was a geek who thought he was way cooler than he was. . . . But I liked him.

And I wasn't aiming low with Baron, as I had once believed. He was intelligent, caring, handsome, and he wasn't afraid to let his feelings show. Baron Chomsky was a real catch for a girl who wasn't bent on impressing those around her. If I ever saw him again, I was going to let him know. . . . If I ever saw him again.

Nowhere to run to, nowhere to hide.

The double doors swung open.

I peered around the table. Six shadowy zombies entered.

Sensing my presence, the überzombies began searching. I dodged them, crawling from behind one table to another, from shadow to shadow, at times narrowly missing being seen. Eventually the zombies spread out, blanketing the room. They were forcing me toward the rear, where there would be no escape.

Chapter
Thirty-five

 I continued ducking behind tables, narrowly escaping detection by the zombies, but time was running out. In a few moments there would be no tables left to duck behind.

Nowhere to run to, nowhere to hide.

I reached the wall. The zombies inched closer. It was time to make a stand.

I stood up.

"Over here," I called. I meant to say it loudly, bravely, but my quaking words were a near whisper.

"Mmmm." The zombie moan was a few feet away.

"Hhh!" I let out a tiny, involuntary gasp. The zombie six feet from me spun around. "Here I am," I said with a bit more conviction.

The überzombie quickly closed the distance between us and corralled me with arms heavy like cement.

I punched him in the nose.

"Yeee!" he screamed, but he didn't let go. His grip was unrelenting.

The rap on the nose didn't work on überzombies, I guessed. "Way to go, Principal Taft," I said out loud. He had beaten me.

The überzombie's mouth opened hungrily. His lips moved in, and his rancid breath drifted up my nostrils, attacking my senses. The end was near. This time for sure.

When I become a zombie, I'll find Sybil, and we'll roam the school together, best friends forever.

I consoled myself with the peace in that thought. The room began to spin as the zombie's saliva trickled down my shoulder. . . . Then his icy teeth touched my flesh.

Out of the corner of my eye, I saw something zipping across the room at a tremendous speed. It hit us with fierce intensity. I went sprawling to the floor, but the thing had latched onto the zombie, and they went airborne, traveling twenty feet through the air before crashing into a wall. They slid to the floor. The thing rose, standing over the zombie. It let out a ferocious wail. "*Aiiiiiiiiii!*"

The thing was Sybil. Her complexion was kelly green, her rage-filled eyes a crimson sea.

Slowly, the überzombie got up. He was joined by the others. Sybil bared her zombie teeth as they surrounded her. Not once did she look in my direction, but I knew I had been right. Even as a zombie, she wouldn't attack me. Her sense memories were of an abiding friendship that would last forever.

As the überzombies moved in, she crouched low, like a lioness ready to pounce. I didn't wait to see the fight. I understood what I needed to do. Sybil had saved me so that I could save her. I slipped out of the cafeteria. The attack was vicious—growls and screams, and the sound of ripping flesh.

I cried like a baby as I headed for the subbasement. Moving

away from the ferocious battle, I thought of all the wonderful things Sybil had done for me over the years. But this took the cake. My throat ached as I sobbed out loud. I did not look back.

I pulled open the door leading to the subbasement. The moment I did, I heard the most unwelcome sound. More zombies. Loud zombie moans and shrieks were coming from down the stairs. I peered down the darkened staircase. *There must be hundreds of them down there*, I thought. Then I remembered Sybil, and started down.

I reached the bottom. Before me lay a long, narrow corridor with deeply creviced walls. The corridor, lit only by a few low-wattage bulbs, was empty.

"*Woooooeeeeeohh!*" A zombie wailed from somewhere up ahead. My legs were shaking as I continued in the direction of the sound. There was a door at the end. The boiler room.

The sounds were getting louder.

"Where are they?" I whispered. It was as if the corridor was crawling with zombies, and yet I didn't see any.

"*Oooooooooh!*" I jumped. The sound was just above me. I looked up and spotted the ventilating duct vent. The zombie moans and cries were carrying from upstairs through the duct. There were no zombies here.

"Oh, my goodness," I whispered as I slumped against the wall. I let out a long, slow sigh of relief. I was safe . . . for now.

I reached the door at the end of the corridor. A sign on the old metal door read:

BOILER ROOM
Custodial Staff Only!

I held my breath, and pushed in.

The boiler room was as dimly lit as the corridor. As I entered, I was assailed by the dank and pungent odor of mold and mildew.

Baron and Milton were seated in folding chairs across the room in front of the huge metal boiler. They didn't see me at first, but as I stepped into the room, their heads lifted. Slowly, both boys rose. Baron's lips parted.

"Hello, beautiful."

I couldn't believe my ears.

"What are you doing here?" chimed Milton.

My eyes widened. "You're not zombies. You're not zombies!" I cried as my heart sang out with relief. I raced across the room, threw my arms around Milton, who was the closest to me, and hugged him.

"Get offa me!" he squawked. "Of course we're not zombies." He pushed me away.

"Is someone gonna hug *me*?" Baron asked.

I looked into his smiling eyes and threw my arms around him.

"That's what I'm talkin' about," he said, grinning. I thought I'd never see that smile again.

"What are you doing here?" Milton again.

"I came for the antidote. What are *you* doing here?"

Baron explained that when Principal Taft stumbled upon their lab, he was so happy to discover what they were doing, he officially enlisted them to create the new antidote. He brought them here, where they could work undetected.

"So, you're not prisoners?" I said.

"Course not. We're free as birds. We go home every night," said Milton.

"And every day we work on the new antidote. It'll be ready in a few days," added Baron.

"We don't have that long," I said gravely. "Besides, as soon as you give him the antidote, he's going to turn you into zombies."

I told them the entire story. "He doesn't want to turn the students back. That would spoil his plan. The only reason he wants an antidote is insurance in case he ever needs it."

As the meaning behind what I'd said sank in, Baron and Milton started getting angry.

Milton pounded his fists into his thighs. "He suckered us!" he snapped. "I told you not to trust him!"

"No, you didn't. You said he was going to make us superstars."

"Oh. Right. Dude, if only the original antidote had worked, we *would* be superstars."

"Maybe it did." The words drifted up from deep in my soul. Baron and Milton turned to me, and I spoke the truth I'd been hanging on to for so long. "You were right. I didn't use it on Dirk."

"I knew it!" cried Milton, jumping up and down.

"Chill, dude!" A stunned Baron turned to me. "Why?" he asked. "I trusted you."

"I know." I heard the betrayal in his voice, and wished I could hide somewhere under a rock.

"I was afraid if Dirk turned back he wouldn't be my boyfriend anymore. I'm so sorry." My voice cracked, and yet there was a welcome weightlessness about me as I unburdened myself with the truth.

"It's okay," Baron said tenderly.

"No, it's not okay!" Milton blurted. "We could have been heroes already."

"He's right. I betrayed your trust," I said.

Baron looked into my eyes and nodded. "Yes, you did," he said. "But it sounds like you've been beating yourself up over this. No sense in us beating you up, too."

"It was so stupid of me. The boy of my dreams was right in front of me, and I was wasting my time trying to be like . . . Amanda."

Baron perked up. "Boy of your dreams? Who's that?"

"Who do ya think?" I held my breath, looked into his gorgeous hazel eyes, waiting for a response.

A Cheshire cat grin appeared on his face. "*Moi?*" he asked.

I nodded. "I'm really sorry, Baron."

"I forgive you."

"Well, I don't!" Milton screeched.

"Milton! Can't you see me and Margot are having a moment here?" His eyes bored into Milton. It was probably the harshest he'd ever sounded to his friend. Milton quieted.

He turned back to me. "He forgives you, too. He's just having a hard time showing it right now."

"You held Sybil's hand," I suddenly said. The hurt I'd felt seeing them that day in the pit room was still there.

Baron's grin turned sheepish. "Just trying to get your attention, beautiful."

"Well, you got it," I said. I moved in and kissed him on the mouth—and he kissed back. His lips were warm and soft against mine. My first *real* kiss, with a boy I cared about. My heart fluttered . . . fortunately my stomach did not.

Thunk . . . Thunk . . .

Someone was knocking at the boiler room door. We three faced the door and realized it wasn't knocking. Zombies were throwing their bodies against the door. The zombies had found us.

"Do you have any more of the original antidote?" I asked, hoping Principal Taft had lied.

"Yeah, plenty," said Milton.

"Great! Excellent! If we can squirt it into their mouths, we can turn them back to normal."

"We don't even know if it works," said Baron.

"I believe in it. I believe in you." I turned to Milton. "Where is it?"

"At home."

"Dude!" cried Baron.

Milton stamped his foot like a child. "She said it didn't work!"

"Are you sure you have a four-point-oh GPA?" asked Baron.

"She said it didn't work!" Milton squawked.

Thunk . . . Thunk . . .

"Guys, pretty soon they're going to figure out how to open that door. We've gotta get out of here."

"There is no other way out," said Milton. He stared at the door.

I looked up. In the wall, high above us, was the grate to the ventilation duct.

"Yes, there is." I climbed up onto a chair. As I began fiddling with the grate over the duct, my ankle roared with pain. "I need some help here."

"Manual labor is not my thing," said Milton.

Baron sighed. "We should leave him behind." He got on the chair, standing next to me. The touch of his skin against mine sent waves of icy chills dancing along my arms, giving me gooseflesh. His touch was electric.

How come I never noticed it before?

He removed the grate. It dropped to the floor with a loud clang.

"Now what?" called Milton, eyeing the opening in the wall with trepidation.

"We exit through the ventilating ducts," I replied.

"We don't know what's in there. We don't even know where it goes." Milton's eyes were still on the opening.

Thunk . . .

The door was starting to give.

"You're right, Milton," I said, a soft urging in my voice. "But it's our only chance. If we stay, the zombies will get us. But if we're able to get to the antidote, you'll be a hero."

He brightened a little.

"I guess," he said. He still wasn't certain about my plan. But we had to try it.

Baron helped me into the duct. Then he and Milton shimmied in after me. The zombie sounds were louder here, as if the ducts were teeming with zombies. But I knew better . . . at least, I hoped I did.

Chapter

Thirty-six

We started crawling through the duct.

"Okay, now what?" called Milton, who was bringing up the rear.

"If we can make it to Principal Taft's office, I have an idea how we can subdue them long enough for us to escape the building."

I scrambled up, into dusty darkness. It was a grueling climb. The duct was cramped and stuffy. There was very little air. After about fifteen minutes we came to a bend. "I think this is the basement. We have to go up one more floor."

Shimmying upward in a duct is no easy task. You have to push up against the sides with your feet, using your arms to brace yourself. It's easy to lose traction, and you can slip backward several feet and have to start all over again. It took us nearly half an hour to reach the first floor.

As I shimmied I thought of Mrs. Mars. I'd had no idea there was a practical use for all that upper-body training she was always trying to get us to do. I guess she realized girls needed to be prepared for whatever unexpected dilemma life threw at us.

Why didn't she just say that?

I was breathing hard, sweat pouring down my arms and legs. "The rest should be easy," I said. "No more climbing."

The duct wrapped around the entire first floor. Several smaller ducts led off the main duct into the classrooms.

"Is this our first date?" Baron suddenly called from behind.

I smiled. "You're not getting off that easy. We're going out in public."

"You won't be embarrassed to be seen with a geek?" he asked.

Seven weeks ago the answer would have been yes.

"You're not a geek," I replied. Then I said, "You won't be embarrassed to be seen with a nobody?"

"You're not a nobody."

I immediately thought of Sybil's attempts to do away with the cliques and their labels. Lunchroom monitor wasn't a ridiculous idea after all.

"Could you guys please shut up!" Milton called from the rear. "This is like watching a love story. And I hate love stories . . . unless somebody dies."

We continued on in silence. I stopped at one point and looked through the grate, just to make sure we were headed in the right direction. I peered into the corridor. Zombies were everywhere.

"*Achoo!*" Milton sneezed.

"Dude!" Baron smacked him on the shoulder.

The zombies all snapped out of their fugue, looking hungrily upward. But their virus-fogged brains couldn't figure out where the sneeze had come from, and eventually they went back to shuffling along the corridor.

We arrived at a duct veering off to our left.

"This should be the main office," I said.

We crawled into the duct. When we arrived at the next grate, I again peered through. We were indeed above the main office.

The six überzombies were in the office.

"Those are the überzombies," I whispered. "This is probably where Taft stages them." The zombies stood almost motionless. Their eyelids were near shut, as if they were sleeping, but I knew better. These were the most deadly zombies in the school.

Baron inched up alongside me and looked through the vent. His hand brushed my arm—again my skin turned to gooseflesh. "Tyler Moss," he whispered.

"I tutored him in algebra," said Milton from the rear. "He got a B plus, thanks to me."

"I don't think you're going to get any points for that today," I said.

We continued into the duct leading into Taft's office. The door to Taft's office was always closed. Hopefully we'd find the office empty.

I looked through the grate. The office was empty.

"We're in luck," I called. I shifted my body around so that my feet were in front of the grate. I gave three hard kicks, and the grate popped out, crashing to the floor.

That would attract some zombie attention.

I looked down into Taft's office, listening intently.

"I don't think they heard it."

"Be careful," called Baron.

He squeezed my hand; then I jumped down, landing hard on the floor. Pain fired through my ankle. "*Aiii!*" I cried.

My eyes moved to the door. We held our collective breaths, waiting for zombies to come barreling into the room.

"We're good," I called, releasing my breath.

Baron jumped down after me, and then Milton.

"I need one of you to hook Sybil's iPod up to the intercom system," I said.

"Piece of cake," said Milton. Having something to do would keep his mind occupied, and his fear at bay. I pulled Sybil's iPod from my pocket and handed it to him. He went right to work.

Just then the doorknob turned.

"Hurry!" I called. "Überzombies know how to open doors."

Baron rushed to the door, but it was too late. It was already swinging open.

"Mmmmm," was all we heard from the other side. The überzombies had come to life.

Baron braced himself against the door. "Little help," he called.

"Hurry!" I called to Milton again.

In seconds the iPod was plugged into the system. I cued up Tom Jones' "She's a Lady," and hit the play button. Then, Milton and I joined Baron at the door. We leaned our shoulders into it, against the relentless zombies.

The music started to play.

"We crawled all the way here for pansy music?" asked Milton. "At least you could have played some Sid Vicious."

"Hey, hey! Trust me here. I've got a two-point-seven GPA," I responded.

"We're dead."

As Tom Jones' melodious voice resounded throughout the school, the pushing against the door abruptly stopped. Angry growls sprang up on the other side.

"What's happening?"

"They don't like Tom Jones, either. A few weeks ago Sybil played this song in the lunchroom, and all the zombies went berserk."

"Just what we need—berserk zombies," said Milton.

"I turned it off before anything happened, but I have a feeling they would have done anything to get out of there."

Baron smiled. "That's my girl."

We peeled back the door and peeked into the main office. The zombies were acting strange. They had begun walking in aimless circles.

One by one they began to scream.

"*Yeeeee!*" They swatted at their ears, and shook their heads as if there was a bee buzzing inside and they were trying to get it out. The happy beat that always cheered me and Sybil up was having a horrible effect on them.

"*Yeee-e-e-e-ooo.*" The screeching slowed.

"They're dying," said Milton, astonished.

It seemed to be true. Not only did the screeching slow, but their movements became more and more sluggish. And then one by one, the zombies stopped. Like the Tin Man from *The Wizard of Oz*, who'd rusted in the rain, they stood frozen in place. The happy music had short-circuited their brains. A room full of überzombies now stood motionless, harmless, their dark eyes staring into space, as the voice of Tom Jones filled the air.

"You did it," Baron cried.

"*We* did it," corrected Milton.

I smiled. "You guys can have all the credit. You deserve it."

We exited Principal Taft's office and picked our way around the lifeless zombies in the outer office. Stepping out into the main corridor, we observed more of the same—a sea of motionless zombies.

We began moving through, making our way to the exit.

"Look out!" Milton called.

We turned in time to see one of the zombies who had been unaffected by the music coming for us.

My voice cracked when I saw who it was. Sybil. "This one's with me," I said.

A jagged scratch ran down her cheek. Her face was bruised, and her clothing had been ripped in the lunchroom battle with the überzombies. I took her hand. It was cold.

"Thanks," I whispered. "You saved me. Now, we're going to save you." There were tears in my eyes.

"Let's get out of here," Milton called.

We again began heading for the main exit door when I remembered it had been chained shut. "Uh-oh. Do either of you know where we might find a bolt cutter?"

"I do," said Milton.

"Great! You guys are always prepared. Where is it?"

"It's at home," said Milton.

"Dude!" Baron walloped him in the back of the head.

Chapter
Thirty-seven

Baron found a hammer in the janitor's closet, and after several whacks the lock on the chained exit surrendered, and we were free. I took Sybil back to my house, where I was surprised to find Dirk still in my living room, in front of the TV. My parents had already gone to bed. Dirk sat alone, staring at an infomercial featuring a ladder that could do more tricks than a trained seal.

The night had been a disaster with one bright spot—Baron and Milton were safe, and they had the antidote.... Okay, three bright spots.

I limped into the kitchen, dumped an ice tray into a Baggie, and made an ice pack for my throbbing ankle. Then I joined Dirk on the couch. I looked at him staring at the TV and realized I was about to do something I had never thought I was capable of.

"Umm, Dirk. We need to talk," I said softly.

Slowly his eyes moved to me. His head cocked to one side.

"These past couple of months have been wonderful. Really wonderful. I've learned so much about myself, about boyfriends, and friendship, and honesty. I couldn't have done any of it without you."

"Mmmmm." A low moan purred deep in his chest.

"But Dirk, I have to break up with you. I thought having a cool boyfriend would make me special. It didn't. If anything, it made me a bigger jerk than I already was. Hey, don't get me wrong, it's not that I don't want a boyfriend. I'm still a healthy sixteen-year-old—of course I do. And I have just the person in mind—someone who isn't into cliques, or being at the top of the social food chain, someone who appreciates me for me, which most of the time isn't all that good, but I'm working on it. Anyway, sorry, but we're through. I hope you understand."

I leaned in and kissed him on his crumbly green cheek. Dirk looked at me, and I thought I saw something finally register on his face—recognition, understanding. I thought that I had cut through the thick zombie fog in his mind, and he knew exactly what I was saying . . . until he tried to bite my face off.

Swat!

"Yeeee!"

I turned and looked at Sybil, who sat silently waiting, her breath coming in gravelly gasps, her dark eyes staring into the future. Since the eighth grade, Sybil had been the best friend a girl could have. She'd dealt with all my snarkiness, my desire to be like Amanda Culpepper, and my stupid manifesto. And despite what a lousy friend I'd been, she'd saved my life. Now it was my turn.

"In a little while the boys will bring the antidote over," I told Sybil. "I'll give it to you on a snickerdoodle—your favorite. Then we'll go to my room like we always do. I'll put on some Tom Jones music, get out the nail polish. And we'll sit on my bed, and plan out the rest of our fabulous high school careers."

Epilogue

 The antidote worked.

Baron and Milton brought it over later that night. We gave it to Sybil, and I held my breath. Within a few hours she was back to her old self. When she was normal again I threw my arms around her, breathing for what seemed to be the first time in an eternity.

I hugged her for a full minute.

"Margot, stop!" she whined, squirming in my grasp. Her face turned a bright red as she eyed Baron and Milton. "You're embarrassing me."

I didn't care. "Tough," I said, and continued to hug. I knew even after I released her, ours was a friendship I would never let go of.

Over the next several days Baron and Milton administered the antidote to everyone who had become a zombie, and changed them all back—even Amanda Culpepper.

The students and adults who had become zombies didn't remember much. It was as if they'd been asleep for an entire semester. And by the time winter break was over, things in our town had gotten back to normal.

I hadn't seen Mrs. Mars since they changed her back, but I was looking forward to my semester in her class. No more bleachers and excuse notes for me.

To Sybil's dismay, the popular kids went back to being popular, the slugs went back to being slugs, and everyone migrated back into their tight-knit groups, just like before.

Baron and Milton never got to be the Big Dogs they'd dreamed of becoming. But Baron did get something for all his troubles—a girlfriend. Me.

For my part, I finally realized the cool kids weren't the ones with the best wardrobes, or the best figures, or even glacier-blue eyes. They were the kids with the best attitudes.

Principal Taft never came back to school. He vanished, as if into thin air. When the spring semester began, a new principal, Mr. Fargas, took over.

The Saturday before spring semester was to begin, I invited Sybil to my house. When she arrived, I pulled out my manifesto.

"Oh, my goodness," she said, snatching the page from my hand and ripping it in half.

"What are you doing?"

"Isn't that why you pulled it out? This manifesto has caused us nothing but trouble. We need to get rid of it." She placed the two halves together and prepared to rip them again.

"Stop!" I called. "I like having the manifesto." I snatched it back and began looking for some tape to patch it back together.

"But last semester was a fiasco."

"I know, but the problem wasn't the manifesto, Sybil. The problem was me. I still want to be popular, I still want to go to parties, and I still want a boyfriend . . . well, actually I have a boyfriend. So the semester wasn't a total failure." I smiled. "But more importantly, I never again want to sacrifice my relationship with my friends to get the things I want." I taped the manifesto back together. "I'm keeping this as a reminder."

I moved to my dresser, where I picked up a tiny, brightly wrapped package and handed it to her.

"What's that for?"

"For you."

"What's the occasion? It's not my birthday. Do you know something that I don't know? Am I getting expelled?"

"Sybil!" I smiled. "Do I need a special occasion to give a present to my very best friend?"

An odd expression crossed her face as she looked at me for a moment. "Absolutely not," she replied. She took the package, ripped into it, and pulled out the charm bracelet I had picked out especially for her. There was a single charm hanging from a link on the bracelet. A tree.

A warm smile crossed her lips. "It's beautiful." For a moment I thought she was going to cry.

"It's in honor of when I met my best friend," I said.

"I know." Her voice was cracking as she put on the bracelet. "Thank you," she said, admiring it on her wrist.

Just then: "Hey, Margot, what are you guys doing in there? Mom says you have to take me to the mall for new sneaks. Pronto!" called Theo.

"All right!" I said with an exasperated sigh.

I recalled the evening when I'd first started dating zombie Dirk. Theo had come to my bedroom door to annoy me, and I'd flirted with the idea of yanking the door open, tying a leg of lamb around his scrawny neck, and letting Dirk have at him.

Gosh, I wish I had.

Cranford College
Office of Admissions
3501 Trousdale Pkwy
Room #101A
Amherst, MA 01002

Dear Miss Johnson,

Congratulations! Let me be the first to welcome you to the fall freshman class of Cranford College. I enjoyed reading your essay. My, what a wonderful imagination you have. It was quite clever how you used zombies to describe your journey through high school. I believe you are just the kind of thoughtful and engaged student that will benefit from the Cranford experience.

I took the liberty of passing your essay along to the head of our creative writing department. I told her I think we have a female Stephen King on our hands.

I am very pleased to hear that you and entering freshman Sybil Mulcahy have already taken the initiative to start a Save the Planet Club at Cranford. It shows just the kind of motivation we enjoy in our students. I look forward to meeting you both in the fall.

Very truly yours,

Lloyd B. Bartlett

Lloyd Baskins Bartlett
Dean of Admissions,
Cranford College

Acknowledgments

I'd like to thank my agent, Jim Kellem, for making this possible; my manager, Sheree Guitar, for her unfailing belief in me, and for providing a venue for the readings; Garett and Yvette, for listening to the early chapters; Latif, whom I first ran the idea past, and who told me to go for it; Lorraine, who puts up with so much; and special thanks to Susan, editor extraordinaire, who helped find the soul in a silly story.